so far gone

so far gone

A NOVEL BY
PAUL CODY

PICADOR USA
NEW YORK

Picador® is a U.S. registered trademark and is used by St. Martin's Press under license from Pan Books Limited.

Design by Maureen Troy

Library of Congress Cataloging-in-Publication Data

Cody, Paul.
      So far gone / by Paul Cody — 1st Picador USA ed.
         p.   cm.
      ISBN 0-312-18180-9
      I. Title.
   PS3553.0335S6   1998
   813' .54—dc21   97-33371
                                                            CIP

First Picador USA Edition: February 1998

10   9   8   7   6   5   4   3   2   1

For my teachers: Robert Abboud and Charles Vallely;
John Mack and Bill Schickel; Martha Collins;
Stephanie Vaughn; Peggy Dieter; and the ideal,
genuine men—Gould Colman and Lamar Herrin.
With thanks and love.

ACKNOWLEDGMENTS

Many thanks and candles lit to my friends and readers, Will Evans, Chet Frederick, Brian Hall, Ed Hardy, Teresa Jesionowski, Peter Landesman, John Lauricella, Steve Madden, Steve Marion, Dan McCall, Stewart O'Nan, Micah Perks, and Julie Schumacher. Thanks to my wife, Liz Holmes, for reading and rereading, editing, listening, and for keeping two redheaded boys at bay. And to my agent, Sloan Harris, for his civility, sense, and stout heart; and to George Witte at Picador for his discerning dark taste. I owe much to Richard Selzer's essay about his stay with Benedictine monks, and to Stephen Trombley's *The Execution Protocol* for the particulars of lethal injections. Thanks to the English Department at U. Mass/Boston, the graduate writing program at Cornell University, the New York Foundation for the Arts, and to my spiritual guides/monster walkers/fellow travelers—Manette Ansay, Burl Barr, C. A. Carlson, C. N. Hetzner, Bob Lautenslager, Beth Saulnier, and Harry Segal. And especially, thanks and longing to the memories of Jack and Michele.

We tell ourselves stories in order to live.
　　　　　　　　—JOAN DIDION
　　　　　　　The White Album

It was Frederick's understanding that the prisoners had a story: that each night for months, at nine precisely, a light had burned in a window in the town, where the men on one cellblock's upper tier could see it and wonder, and imagine, each one, that it shone for him alone. But that was just a story, something that people will tell themselves, something to pass the time it takes for the violence inside a man to wear him away, or to be consumed itself, depending on who is the candle and who is the light.
　　　　　　　　—DENIS JOHNSON
　　　　　　　　Angels

For Mercy has a human heart,
Pity, a human face,
And Love, the human form divine,
And Peace, the human dress.
　　　　　　　　—WILLIAM BLAKE
　　　　　　Songs of Innocence

so far gone

1.

THEY ONLY LOOK at me sometimes. To push in the tray of food or for medicine every three or four hours.

Then each day, I think, maybe every second or third day, Father Curran comes along and they take me to the room where I talk to him. Plastic chairs, and no windows, and the table that seems like wood but is really just something made to appear that way.

They have the belt around my middle and the cuffs chained to the belt, and more chains on my ankles, so my arms and legs won't move too much. And maybe that's how I will be when they come for me not long after midnight, when they say, Okay, you. It's time now. And all of us—Father Curran and two or three or four of them—will walk down the concrete halls. Moving slowly and for the last time.

Father Curran has watery blue eyes that are yellow around the edges like nicotine stains, and skin that is tired and wrinkled. He puts his hand on my shoulder and calls me Son. Let us pray, he says, and he looks in my eyes and then down at his lap.

He wears a gray sweater over his black shirt, and has the white collar in front. There is a small brown stain on the arm of the sweater, like rust or dried blood or something.

Perpetual light shine upon them, he says, his lips moving almost silently, and the words hiss and whisper, soft like that.

There are long tubes of light overhead, and the sounds don't echo so much in here the way they do everywhere else.

Our Father, who art in heaven, he whispers, and his tired eyes are closed and resting, and on the eyelids there are faint red and blue veins like a road map. Father Curran has traveled a long way to be here, over hills, past rivers and farms.

As it was in the beginning, he whispers, is now and ever shall be, and his voice is like water lapping in a bath, the room full of steam and the tiles sweating, and everything calm like sleep and quiet and a soft pillow.

Time, a man says, and we stand up, and walk slowly out and down the hall.

I'm light as air by now and very very tired, and I would not be here if it was not meant to be. These places are not full of Boy Scouts and altar boys and innocent men, so I shouldn't begin to think that way.

The concrete is gray like a battleship, and somewhere, a long time ago, something bad happened.

If I say what it was and ask forgiveness and accept into my heart the kingdom, the day and time, then all things can be as one once again.

And back in here I lie down still again—for more hours and days and nights. They will bring a second white pill and a green pill and a tan capsule. The lights are out for a while—and once, a long time ago, there was someone who said, Jack, so soft in my ear, and I could feel her breath, and then we were laughing, then everything was quiet.

Maybe there were oak trees swaying over us in the breeze. Maybe wind in the branches, and the stars far away beyond the very top of the trees and the sky. More stars than we had ever seen.

This is how we will be, she said. Her name was Ellen. It was Jessica and Alison and Jodie.

Then a dog was barking, and for a long time something was wrong. Someone was very angry. Someone had an urge. A strong, strong urge to do something. And the air would get quiet and the urge wouldn't go away.

So I was out at night. Sipping from a pint bottle of gin or rum. So much heat in the chest, in the belly, going down, then spreading all over. And seeing the streets in Newton, Massachusetts, in the neighborhoods with big houses.

Put down everything, Father Curran said. From as far back and no matter how unimportant and every scrap and shred and shard. And from that, piece by piece by piece—maybe something, some pattern or picture or thing will begin to emerge.

Like something you heard whispered way back, or some smell of bread as you walked past the bakery on a winter morning on your way to church.

Because what happens in May, what they will do after we walk slowly down the halls, and through metal doors, past people who look on with a kind of awe, and into a room with blinds on the windows and seats on the other side for people to sit and watch—what they will do is erase all of that, and there will be nothing here for us anymore. Only a long silence. A great loneliness.

But first the man hands in the small white cup with a tan capsule, and I swallow that, and he does not look at me at all. Just down at my hands. Then he goes away.

This is what I have. Two boxes of books. Eight notebooks, three pencils, slippers, a metal toilet and mirror, the cot that is attached to the wall. It has a blanket, a pillow, a thin mattress covered with rubber.

There are my hands and they tremble and move when I try to keep them steady, then nothing.

Write a prayer down, if nothing else, he said. Write, Our Father, who art in heaven. Or something like that.

Hallowed be, and so forth.

Sometimes there are veils in front of my face, and bits of smoke and fog. There are curtains I can't quite see through. I see a shadow sometimes, and I lie down and hold my head in my hands, and I can feel all the heat in there, like wheels and belts and pistons, going so fast, and no oil left, and all of it getting hotter and hotter until smoke seems to rise from my head.

Once upon a time, I start, in a place a long way from here, in a time that few remember, there was a little boy. A boy in a dreamy place. That is how so many stories begin.

2.

THEY HOVERED OVER him like whispers and dreams. They moved without walking. They had blond hair and black hair and hair that was almost red. They spoke so softly, he often wondered if he had really heard them.

Little boy, they said. Sweet little boy.

They called him, Peanut. Pumpkin. Possum.

They wore white uniforms, and some of them wore blue or green or red cardigan sweaters over their uniforms. They had watches and stethoscopes, and they touched his wrist, his forehead, the side of his face.

You'll be fine, they said. A little while longer.

Hold on, they told him.

Their voices were a warm breeze, a song, a blanket at night.

He never moved except to open and close his eyes, and to lick his lips, and every once in a while to move his fingers or his toes.

First it was night and then day. It was early in the morning and then mid-afternoon, and he thought there was sun outside, or clouds, or the moon and stars.

There were blips and pings and faint dripping sounds. Maybe it was raining out, and he imagined the millions of drops of rain falling everywhere, drumming on roofs and in gutters, and slapping the leaves on bushes and trees, and then rain falling in the streets of the city late at night.

The whole world shines, he thought. Everything glistens like stores at Christmas.

Then he blinked his eyes and the one with brown hair was standing there. She wore glasses that made her face look like the headlights of a car, and her hair was falling forward and swaying, and there were hints of red in her hair.

She lifted his arm in her hands and said, This will be cold. You'll feel something like ice on the inside of your elbow.

She touched him there with cotton, and it was cold. It was snow, only it was just a feeling.

Now you'll feel a pinch, she said, and it did pinch, and then it was something sharp and hot. Something almost pulling at his vein.

Okay, she said. There you go, buddy, she said.

The needle was out of his arm, and she put a cap on the point of the needle, and she felt at the inside of his wrist.

She looked at her watch, and he could tell she was counting.

His arm still hurt, still pinched and stung, but it was like a car backfiring two streets over. He could hear it, but it was somewhere else too.

She said, Today is Saturday. I want you to know that.

She wrote something on a clipboard.

It's 12:23 in the afternoon, she said.

She put the back of her fingers on his cheek.

This is February thirteen, and outside it's about thirty degrees and there's a lot of snow on the ground.

I want you to know that, pal, she said. It's Saturday, she said again. It's February thirteen.

Then he was off in some ocean. He was drifting and floating. The top of his brain was very cold. It was air and ice and far far stars. He was twirling slowly around, and he thought he heard voices saying, Jackie.

Jackie, c'mere, they said, and then someone was laughing.

An old lady like Gramma was there with her thick glasses and her big hands. She held him by the wrist and she was saying, You're a good boy, Jackie. You're a good boy.

What's happened to you? she said, and an old man like Grandpa was sitting in his rocking chair on the front porch, and he was sucking on his pipe. It smelled like burning leaves. He wore reading glasses, and he had a tooth missing.

A voice on an intercom said, Dr. Bruce, line two-nine-nine, please. Dr. Bruce, line two-nine-nine.

A man wearing a tie was standing over him, and the man tapped his chest and pressed at his belly, and felt at the sides of his neck and then along the top and back of his head.

They put a pillow under his head. The pillow was cool at first, but later it was warm, and they put another blanket over him.

Then a woman with blond hair was sitting on the side of the bed, and she was holding a cup with a straw to his mouth, and it was orange juice and was sweet.

It took a long time to drink the juice. There was ice in the cup, and the juice kept dribbling down the side of his mouth, and the lady with blond hair said, That's okay, possum.

He could stay quiet a long time. He didn't have to move ever again.

Nobody could come in and tell him to move or do anything for a long while.

He could be as still as a dead person on television. As still as a cat he saw on the side of the road, blood dripping from its mouth.

Hail Mary, full of grace, he whispered to himself. Blessed art thou.

Now and at the hour of our death, he thought.

Just quiet and careful all the time, he thought.

He was in a car, and someone was driving. Maybe it was a young beautiful lady or maybe it was an old lady. Maybe it was someone he didn't know or see at all. They were driving fast, and the car was shaking, and he watched the dial go from thirty to forty to fifty to sixty to seventy, and he said, Please, please, please, and she was laughing.

The young lady, his mom, was laughing, or the old lady, his gramma, was laughing, and then he was in the bedroom, he was hiding under the bed. In the next room music was playing. Perry Como was singing, and the walls were dark, and Mom was laughing and Dad was laughing.

Dad had red hair, and his breath was minty, and he liked to come home from work and sit in a chair at the kitchen table and read the newspaper in peace.

You be quiet, Jack, Mom said. You just try to keep it down, young man, Mom said.

They were sitting on the back porch and the night was thick and slow. So hot you could fry an egg on the sidewalk, Dad said.

Dad said, When I was your age, I used to deliver newspapers to help my mom out. I used to sweep floors and find bottles because they were worth two cents. We were happy when we found a few bottles. We bought red hots and fire balls and giant pretzels.

Mom sipped and Dad sipped, and the crickets were in the grass making noise.

If you tried hard and were good, then Jesus and God and everyone else would love you very much.

How come? he asked, and Mom said, Because God wants only what's good for you.

Dad said, This, that, whatever.

So many things happened so fast he didn't know what was what, or where anything began or ended, and they were coming up to him when he was asleep. They pulled the covers up to his neck, and he could feel them looking at him, and he pressed his eyelids even more tightly closed.

The woman in white said she was very very sorry. Her eyes were wet.

Gramma had big glasses, and she was Dad's mother, and she had hands like the roots of a tree. She was standing in the doorway, and she said, Where did you come from? And Grandpa, the old man, was smiling, sitting at the kitchen table.

He was blowing a smoke ring at the light in the ceiling.

Gramma put her hand on his shoulder, and she said, Sometimes I look up and there you are, like an Indian. Quiet as an Indian.

Pumpkin, the woman in the blue cardigan said, and she leaned close to the side of his face and said, Hush.

Shhh, she whispered. Nobody will hurt you. Nobody will touch you.

So now he was quiet as night, and he wouldn't say anything, and no matter what they said or did, he'd lie there, and nobody could come near him anymore. Not with lights or needles or anything.

He opened his eyes and saw white tubes of light on the ceiling, and tiles that had tiny holes in them. He counted seven rows of tile, and then he began to count the holes, and he wondered if there were as many holes in the tiles as stars in the sky and grains of sand in the sandbox at the park.

The park was surrounded by tall trees, and the sunlight couldn't fall down through the leaves. He always tried to look up, and the highest branches were nearly in heaven, up close to the sun and the white puffs of clouds. It made him dizzy to lean so far back and look for so long. He felt he would spin around and around, and he would become sick.

Something went by in the hall, and when he turned to look, it was already gone, and he needed to scratch his side, and his leg, right above the knee.

Then they were wheeling him down a hallway, and all the people they passed were tall as trees. They smiled at him, and a woman with gray hair patted his arm.

Nice little boy, she said, and then Mom was saying, Jackie. Sweetheart. Honey.

They would fix what was wrong inside him.

There was a rupture and there was infection.

That meant there were germs running all around in his belly, like an army, and that was why he didn't feel so good.

Dr. Heath would fix him. Dr. Kaplan would help too.

Early tomorrow morning, Mom said. Before the birds are even

awake. They would take him to the special room. They would put him to sleep, and he wouldn't feel a thing.

Don't be afraid, the woman with black hair said. Don't worry about a thing.

There was another cold spot and a pinch, this time on his upper arm, near the shoulder, and everything went cold.

He could lie there and be more quiet than an Indian. Gramma wouldn't even know he was there.

Floating on water was like floating across the sky. Like clouds moving so slowly that he couldn't even tell they were moving. Like lying in bed at night, and all of the darkness surrounding him, and the snow falling outside and making a blanket to cover the earth.

Or when he went for a walk with Grandpa, in the streets of the neighborhood. Everybody they saw smiled at them. People sitting on porches, and people walking by. One man was cutting his grass, and that smelled nice. That smelled like summer.

But when it got cold outside, he couldn't walk so far with Grandpa. There was too much ice and snow, and one time Grandpa slipped on the ice and broke his ankle, and that was no fun. That was no fun at all.

So he would have to be patient. He would have to learn to sit still and wait.

He tried to turn over, but he couldn't, and then a woman with a red face and glasses was wiping his forehead with a damp cloth. Then the cloth was on his cheeks and eyes, and it went over his mouth too.

His mouth was dry. He couldn't drink anything or eat anything because they would have to put him to sleep soon, and having even a little something to eat or drink could cause problems. So he would need patience.

And then it would be over and he would feel better.

So how come? he wanted to ask. So what was that for? Why did he get sick? And why did everything feel like pins and needles?

He could see sharp as a bell. A bell rang loud and clear, and the sound hung in the air.

Like the frost in the morning, when the leaves were falling from the trees. And he went out to the backyard and he ran around and around the tree, and the garage spun past, and the house next door raced by, and the house behind their house—it seemed to float up.

Little boy, they said. Sick little boy.

A fever made you hot all over. A fever was like a fire inside of you. A fever made things kind of funny, so he wasn't too sure what was what.

He thought maybe it was late at night, like when he woke up at home, and heard a single clock ticking and tocking and ticking and tocking. He didn't know what would happen if he had to get out of bed and go to the bathroom.

The light from the moon made milky squares on the floor, and later, on the wall. A car passed by out on the street and he could hear the car for a long time, as it got farther and farther away.

But then it was early, and he was in the hospital, where you went when you got very sick. And maybe it was three or four in the morning, and a woman in white came, and a thin man with pale blue pajamas on, and a cap over his hair, and they had masks like bank robbers on television.

They lifted him to a thin bed that had wheels, and, oh, oh, that hurt so bad in his belly.

That was knives and fire all at once.

They put a sheet over him, and he watched the ceiling. He saw tiles and tubes of light and speakers and the tops of door frames.

Then they stood in front of doors and pushed a button and waited.

I'm Dr. Perkins, a man behind a mask said, and he had a quiet voice. He had a voice that was like a dream. He said, I'll help you go to sleep, and then in a little while, after you're all fixed up, I'll help you wake up.

At first you won't feel so good, Dr. Perkins said, but then you'll feel a little better and a little better still.

Your mom and your dad will be here when you wake up, and you can have something to drink before too long.

First there was a needle in his behind to relax, and he could almost go to sleep already. They were in a white room, with the biggest lights in the world all over the ceiling. They were silver and white, and everyone wore green and blue pajamas, and they were nice to him.

They put his arm on a board, and Dr. Perkins said, You'll feel a pinch, and they put a tube just under his nose for extra air.

He would see God and the angels and they would all have gold circles over their heads. There would be sunshine and fields and flowers. And music all the time. Wavering angel music.

Listen to me count backwards, someone said. A lady with a quiet voice. Count with me if you can. But listen as I count backwards, she said again.

Everyone would be there in heaven. The priest and all the people from church. The people wearing hats and long dark coats and shiny shoes.

One hundred, she said.

Ninety-nine, ninety-eight.

Blip and beep, and something hissed somewhere far away.

When you're gone, someone said.

Far far away.

Ninety-three, ninety-two, she said.

Where the air is clear and birds fly. Where they soar among fleecy clouds.

Fleece as white as snow, and he would be still and quiet, and nobody would do anything anymore to him, and it would not hurt.

Everyone was nice, and Mom and Dad, Gramma and Grandpa, the nice lady with red hair—they were there too. He didn't mind. He was quiet. He was still as stone.

3.

MOSTLY I WAS up that night anyway because it was pretty hot and a Saturday night, Sunday morning, and the cars were going by out on Clifton Street, which is a busy street, especially late on a Saturday night. This is one of the easiest ways to get from Watertown Square to Newtonville or West Newton, or over to Waltham, which is just north of Newton.

The windows up here on the second floor were open, almost all of them anyway, and I had woken up around midnight, which I will do at night just about all the time now that Frank is gone these nine years, ten years come May. The little breezes were blowing in a bit and moving the curtains slowly. They billowed out and looked like ghosts in the darkness, because that is another thing. Very late at night when I wake up and walk around a little in the house, I like to keep the light off. I don't want anyone going by to see the light on and know that this nice old lady who lives alone is up and about and moving around in her nightgown in her house. And God knows I don't want anyone knocking on the door or ringing the doorbell at midnight or two A.M. and saying they're lost and could I tell them how to get to the Mass. Turnpike or to downtown Boston or some such thing. Or they've had an accident or a flat tire and could they come in and use the phone. And what would I say to that? Some big fellow in a dripping raincoat on my front porch, smiling and saying it would just take a minute, won't you let me in, please, ma'am.

On most nights I will go to sleep at around ten or ten-thirty. Drink my tea without the caffeine, and check the locks, and in the winter put the heat down low. And always I will be asleep in a few minutes, and an hour or two later I will be awake, and for a second, just for a second, I will not know where I am. I will think that Frank is on his side of the bed, and Andrea and Pat are in their rooms, and it is thirty-five years ago.

So I wake up and lie there ten or twenty minutes, then I go out to the kitchen, and I walk through the dining room and living room. I look out the windows, at the trees and yards, at the streetlight two houses down on Clifton, and at the Connors' house next door, big and silent and dark. And sometimes I will wander like that, from room to room, chair to chair, for two or three or four hours. Getting my nighttime exercises, I tell Andrea when she calls later.

Then, at four or five, I will go back to bed, and I will fall asleep as easily as one two three. Easy as you please.

The night then, in 1988, was hot. I believe it was late August and I have tried to remember if I heard any commotion before all the things that happened, before all hell broke loose, but I think there was no sound at all. Just the usual cars going by out front—one car, maybe three or four minutes later another car, always going too fast, then crickets and maybe a window or a door somewhere opening or closing, a dog barking off in the distance somewhere, then nothing, then still more nothing.

And I think I looked at the Connors' house, which is three stories tall and big as a ship at sea, and I always thought, It's just closed up and staring. None of the windows open, and sometimes a dim light on some-where deep inside the house—but always that closed, lonely feeling of something sealed off and far away even though it was right there and big and real as life.

So I don't know exactly how it happened. Just that it was Saturday, late on an August night, as I said, maybe around two in the morning. The traffic was getting more scarce, the cars going by maybe one every ten minutes, the whole night getting ready for the long, quiet hush of early Sunday morning. Then I guess I blinked my eyes and there were about ten police cars and ambulances and a fire-rescue truck all over Clifton Street and on Besemer Road across the street, and around the corner on my side, on Chandler Street too.

The lights going around and around, blue and red and blue and red on top of the cars, and the radios inside the cars loud enough to wake the dead saying, Five oh two Clifton, which is the number of the Connors' house, of course, and then some voice would say, Roger, do we need another one?

Then not five minutes later, after the first police cars got there, the station wagons and vans from the television and radio stations in-town were there and they had their lights and cameras and microphones out and switched on.

Maybe two in the morning, maybe two-thirty by then, I guess, and the whole street was stopped up and lit like some movie was going on. Pretty soon there were people standing on the little patches of lawns in front of houses, out front and across the street, at the corner of Besemer, and they're all watching—and inside next door, every light is on in the Connors' house like never before. Like there was a party or a dance or something going on. Bright lights, and flashbulbs from cameras, and I could see the police and the EMT people moving around inside.

Then people are walking around all over my flowers and bushes out front, and they start to walk on my front porch. I hear their steps and I ask myself why with half the Newton police force outside, they can't keep people off some citizen's front porch, then what is wrong, and why do I pay these high taxes?

Before too long the doorbell is ringing, and the phone starts to ring not five or ten minutes later. And mostly for another month or two, it never stopped ringing again. People in the bushes with cameras and microphones, or some reporter in a car out front, writing notes in one of these long skinny notebooks.

What were they like? And what can you tell us about them? And did you ever think in all your life? And what was Jack like? Did he seem like a regular guy? A normal person?

So I hang up the phone and close the door and tell them I don't know. I'm sorry, I can't help you, I say, and I shake my head.

A few times I lied and said I just moved in, not too long ago, and I have no idea who the Connors are or how long they have lived here on Clifton Street. Then I feel as though I should go to Confession and say that I have lied two dozen times or a hundred times.

Because the truth is that I have known them almost forever, since they moved here in 1953, in November, just a month before he, before Jack, was born. Frank and I had been here three years by then. Andrea was five and Pat was almost three, and Joanie was carrying low. The day the truck came with their things, Joanie was so big it looked like she'd have the baby right down there on the walk that ran along the side of their house. She moved slow, and she mostly watched while Bill brought things inside, and Belle and Ed helped carry things too.

So sure, I knew them a long time, since before Jack was born. I guess I've known him all his life, you could say. This little thing. Just a red face in a bundle of blankets, home from the hospital, alive maybe three or four days. Going inside in his mother's arms, a day or two after Christmas. Snow falling, and this life that was just starting.

And now I turn on the television and see his face, and I open the newspaper and there he is, and he will be the first person in Massachusetts in I don't know how many years. To die. To be put to death.

They say on the television that it will happen in another few weeks, just after midnight, down at Walpole at the prison there. All the lawyers are involved, and the governor of course could give him a pardon, and instead he would spend the rest of his life in prison. So every day they show his picture, taken I guess after they arrested him. His hair not too clean, and his face like his face usually looked, only completely different too. Like he was wearing a mask maybe. The way you go into the funeral home and see someone you used to know lying there in a casket. It's them, sure enough. It's the person you used to know. But it's not them too. Something has happened. They've gone somewhere. They're dead, is what they are.

So I see that picture of him, and then they show him walking out of the court after they had decided he was guilty and after he was found not fit to live. His head is bent over like he's trying to duck under a low branch. They have his hands in cuffs, and the cuffs chained to a leather strap at his waist. And there are more chains—thin silver chains—on his ankles too. So he takes little steps like a baby. And on each side of him, and in the front and back of him, are these big state policemen. And even though Jack is a large person, well over six feet and two hundred pounds, he doesn't look so big surrounded by those ones.

Then they show the people from the police, the EMTs and the ones from the coroner's office, taking bodies out on stretchers, the white sheet over the bodies, so you see what looks like a long sack of hay or meal under there. And then it's later and daytime on the film, and there's a picture of the house, the Connors' house, and sometimes, on the side, a piece of my house will be there on the left, if you're looking from the other side of Clifton.

Then they show a picture of Jack from high school that they must have got from the yearbook, and he doesn't look too happy there. Just younger. And there are pictures of the big chair that looks like a dentist's chair where they'll strap him down, and the curtains on the windows of the room there in the prison, and the two or three rows of seats for the witnesses.

Then the camera shows a few people standing across the road from Walpole, or Cedar Junction, as they like to call it now, and they're holding lit candles and a few signs that say, THOU SHALT NOT KILL. Sometimes they'll show a few other people, smiling or looking mad, holding up signs that say, BURN, JACKIE, BURN, or WELCOME TO HELL, JACKIE. Because that's where he would have to go, isn't it? Where else could he go?

All of this, and the trial and the sentence, took place six, seven years ago, and it looks like they're finally going to do it, and they say he does not plan to fight it either. He has made his peace and is ready to go. And I keep thinking of him the day he came home from the hospital. The snow was falling, and Pat and Andrea were standing at the window saying, A baby, a baby.

Then Jack was two or three, and he used to sit in the sandbox that Ed, his grandfather, made next to the garage. Just sitting there hour after hour, pouring the sand through his fingers. And the sun would move across the sky so that in the morning he'd be in the sunshine, but by midday, when it was getting much hotter, the sun would be directly over the garage and he'd be in shade. Belle or Joanie would come out to hang clothes on the line, and they would hardly notice him. For hour after hour it seemed.

Then it was later. He was in school, and he got to be tall, and you never saw him with a friend, and he never said much when you'd see him in the backyard. None of them did. They might nod or smile a little, and you'd see them cutting the grass or bringing groceries in. But you could never get three or four words out of any of them.

Pat and Andrea always said they were weird, but Frank said they just liked to keep to themselves, and there was nothing wrong with that as far as he was concerned.

I guess he did okay in school. He read books all the time. You'd see him coming home from the library with his arms full of books, and sometimes he'd be sitting on the back porch in the sunshine, reading all day, it seemed like. He worked washing dishes, and he painted houses, and I guess he was in and out of the mental hospital a few times. I learned that on the television and in the newspapers. And Bill would go off now and again, move away for a while, and then after not seeing him for what seemed like years, you'd see him in the backyard, carrying groceries inside or washing and waxing a car you'd never seen.

Now I wish I knew, or I think that if only I knew where Bill had gone to and why he had gone away, then I could understand or explain everything. Or sometimes I'd see Jack on the street or in the yard, and he looked fifty pounds thinner, or he was walking slow and careful as an old man. And I'd think, What is wrong there? What happened?

But for the most part, for almost forty years, they were always like that.

Ed Connor died, I think from an embolism, back in the early seventies. He was eighty-two, it said in the paper. He had been a foreman at some kind of plant, and then he worked as a janitor at some private school for boys. He did that until the very end.

Frank and I went to the wake, and there couldn't have been more than eight or ten people in attendance. Belle, Joanie, Bill, and Jack, who was just out of high school, I imagine. And the coffin was closed, and that surprised me. They don't usually do that unless there's been an accident or unless someone had cancer for a year or more and had dropped down to sixty, seventy pounds.

I try to think of him, of Jack Connor, not long before everything happened, maybe when he was working, painting houses or reading his books. They made an apartment on the third floor, and sometimes I heard his car start up late at night. Or I'd hear the car come in very late, and the engine would stop and the car door close.

I'd be up and I'd look out the window. Jack would be standing there in the middle of the backyard. This was maybe three or four in the morning, and he'd just be standing there, not moving. If the moon was bright, I'd be able to see him real clear, and five or ten minutes would go by. I'd want to know what he was looking at and what he was thinking. I'd wonder what kind of person would be up and around at this hour and in all these shadows and this darkness. And then I'd think that he was someone like me. A person who couldn't sleep. A person with nobody to talk to.

And then everything happened, and he was nobody I knew anymore. And the house has been empty ever since.

4.

EVERYTHING WAS NICE up there on the third floor. Everything was just the way I wanted it. I had my radio and TV, my magazines and books. I had my own private entrance, and I could come and go as I pleased. Nobody could stop me.

There were three rooms, the long hallway, and the window at the end of the hall, at the top of the stairs. I could see downtown Boston five or six miles to the east. I could see the top of the Prudential and Hancock buildings, and a cluster of buildings in the financial district. On clear nights, all of Boston seemed to glow and give off heat, like some resting animal.

Just to the north was the Charles River, and from the window the neighborhood there in Newton too. The hedges and roofs. The trees and clotheslines.

Two blocks over was the red brick building, filling most of a block, where I had gone to grade school.

I remembered when my mother brought me that first day for kindergarten, and I screamed and would not let go of her hand. But they made me stay.

That was decades earlier. Then she was downstairs, on the second floor, with my father.

Joanie and Bill, I called them.

Joanie and Bill.

My grandmother lived on the first floor. She was very old, and she was Bill's mother. I called her Belle.

At the end of each month I got a check for my disability. I paid rent, bought food, put gas in my car.

I would shut and lock the door at the bottom of the stairs, and put the radio and TV on low. I'd lie on the couch in the front room, hear the traffic on the street down below.

There was a tree out front, and late in the day the sunshine came through the two windows, lit up the floor and wall, and I thought, I will be here like this for a very long time.

Everything was nice up there. Everything was peaceful.

November was when most of the leaves on the trees had fallen, and then it rained and rained, and the leaves stuck to the sidewalk and streets.

Then the rain stopped and the leaves dried out, and they blew across the pavement. I lay in bed late at night and listened to them, and with covers all around me and the warmth and darkness, I could have been five years old or twelve or twenty-three.

Many things could have been different, and I would turn over, and outside the window the sky was dark, and everything there, in the house, was still.

There were white pills and green pills and yellow pills. They came from the drugstore in brown containers that had white caps, and I kept them lined up on the counter in the kitchen.

I took a green and a white pill in the morning, a white one at noon, green and white ones at dinner, and a yellow pill just before bed.

The walls in there had been white, and the floors were covered by freckled linoleum. The halls were long and led from one dayroom to another.

Everyone wore bathrobes and slippers, and a man sang a song about rainbows and following his dream. Follow, follow, follow, he sang.

Someone said, Shut up. Please, shut up.

Fuck you, someone said. Fuck you very much.

Belle sat in her rocking chair in the den on the first floor, her big hands folded on her lap. She watched television, and said she didn't understand any of the programs anymore.

They're kissing everyone and cheating back and forth, she said.

She looked over at me, her eyes blue behind the thick lenses of her glasses. She said, What about you? Do you know what they're talking about?

Men with men, and girls with girls, she said. It's crazy.

What's wrong with them? she wanted to know.

After the lights were out, I could see dark shapes in the room. I could see a chair, a bureau, a square picture on the wall. I could see a pair of shorts hanging on a nail by the closet door.

Around and slow, I went. Around for a long time. He said not to. He said, Don't.

You little, he said.

You bad bad boy.

I'll fix you, he said. I'll fix you good.

She said, Don't. Please don't.

Around and slow, and he was in the kitchen. Ice cubes clicked, and he said nobody knew the kinds of things he'd seen, and if they knew, they'd think twice before complaining or making judgments.

You don't know, he said. You don't know.

And I was deep down, I was under the covers.

Everything happened at night, and the lights flickered all the time. There were fog and veils.

The sound of everything was loud, then soft, and the light was bright for a second, but everything became dark again. Dark like two or three A.M.

Everything was close and loud, then far away. There was a tick and a ping, and then water dripping slowly, hitting a puddle. A second or a minute later, another drop, then another, and the drops were close by, were near my head.

I curled into myself, and was quiet as dirt.

Don't come near, I thought. Don't come near.

Outside, the sky was big as an ocean. There were stars and clouds and sometimes the moon, and I thought that I would believe in God.

Dear God, I said. Sweet Jesus.

I could believe in God, and I could walk for a long time, past houses that were dark and hulking. The leaves rustled at my feet, they whispered and cooed.

Holy Mary, Mother of God, I prayed. Pray for us sinners, now and at the hour of our death. Amen.

I read books about men who did terrible things, things so scary that sometimes I couldn't sleep after reading about them. In one book, a man wore a cast on his foot and used crutches, and he dropped his books in front of the library, until someone—a young woman with blond hair—stopped to help him.

Where's your car? she asked. Is it far away?

He said, Not too far, and they walked, and when they reached the car, he said he'd give her a ride.

Then he missed the turn, and she said, What? And he said not to be alarmed. Everything would be okay, just be calm.

And they were on a dirt road in the woods, and the trees were all around them, and he said, Get out, and she was crying and saying, No, no, no, no, no.

Dad was small and thin, and he looked at his shoes all the time. He sat at the kitchen table and flipped the channels on the television.

He walked quickly and looked over his shoulder, and said he didn't know anything at all. I just live here, he said.

Don't mind me, he said.

He wore black shoes and a blue sweater that had holes in the elbows. He wore his glasses on a cord that hung around his neck.

You don't say, he said. You're not kidding.

She had brown eyes and her lips were full and red, and when she smiled—when she smiled, her eyes smiled too.

She wore a lavender sweater and gray wool slacks, and she leaned forward and put her hand on my arm, and said, That's okay. Really it is.

She said, That must be nice, and laughed, and the skin at her neck was white, and she took off her glasses, and her eyes—they were brown, and I almost couldn't look at them.

How come? she asked.

Why was that?

Did you feel bad about that?

Tell me, she said.

What was that like?

. . .

Seconds and minutes and hours went by. They ticked and ticked, and some days I could feel every one of them echo over and over.

I used to lean my chin on the windowsill and stare outside. It was cold or hot, the glass had ice on it or the window was open and air blew in. I looked out at the sky and trees, and everything was there, and I would someday go out to see all of it.

Then I was much older, standing in front of the same window, and the sky and air were the same, and the window was no bigger than twenty-five years earlier, but everything else was changed.

Don't do this, I thought. Don't do this anymore, I whispered. And then I wanted to run and shout, wanted to get out somehow from my skin and be some other person in some other place.

Don't do this, I whispered over and over. Don't, don't, don't do this.

More seconds and minutes passed, and I listened and watched, and bit by bit, by and by, I was quiet again. Quiet and still.

The stairs on the way down creaked. The house was old, and groaned in heavy wind, and the radiators clanked and hissed. And as I went down the back stairs, very late, each creak was sharp and loud and I couldn't do anything to make it quiet.

The leaves on the pavement outside rasped and scurried, and they were sleeping. Joanie and Bill, Belle, most of the city. Lying in their beds, in that dark, pale light—in light that made everything glow, in light that looked like heaven.

They all had clocks next to their beds, clocks with faintly lit dials. Red or blue or green numbers, amber light, and everything glowed and ticked past, and they were just lying there on warm sheets, under blankets that surrounded them like a mother's belly.

Their hair spread out over the pillows, an arm flung out, a back sore but resting, a mind at last at ease.

They could sleep for hours and hours. From ten or eleven at night, past midnight, and then to the very darkest, scariest part—after one and two. Deeper and deeper in the dark part of sleep, into the blackest part of night.

The hallway on the second floor was dark. The trash barrel was there, and hooks for coats, and the door that went out to the back porch.

I checked the door to their apartment, to where they lived, and it was locked. Inside would be quiet, I knew. Light from street lamps would be falling, and a table, a lamp, a rocking chair were there, and the two of them were sleeping on each side of the bed.

Down the next set of stairs, past the walls where the plaster was cracked and the stairs didn't creak so much, I felt every breath and every beat of my heart—there at two-thirty in the morning, in that house, with those people.

At the bottom was another trash barrel, and a rug to wipe your feet. There was a door to Belle's, and it was locked when I checked, and then the door to the cellar.

The door to outside opened easily. I slid the bolt, and turned the brass knob, and then the air, the November air, filled me and was tonic.

Houses loomed. Big silent houses all around. A white fence and bushes, and the branches of bare trees. I crossed the backyard in shadow from the moon, and only once, in a single slice, did I pass through direct moonlight between the house and garage.

My car was next to the garage, on the far side, and I unlocked it, got in, smelled the air freshener. Spruce trees, evergreen.

The engine roared to life, then settled to a hum, and I left the lights off as I backed out.

Then I was cruising slowly through blinking red and yellow lights, passing quietly under glowing streetlights, in the shadows of buildings and houses and trees, of all the life that was there.

A car went by on Walnut Street, and a cab sat in Newtonville Square. There were faint interior lights deep within stores, but mostly they were dark and waiting.

I went over a bridge, past more stores, then under more streetlights, past a church, past big houses, parked cars. All of them were quiet, all of them had moonlight washing over their roofs and sides.

They almost whispered and sighed. They almost breathed out and murmured with the pleasure of rest.

At Commonwealth Avenue I went left, up a long hill. The houses were set far back from the street, and had trees and bushes and deep yards surrounding them. I went right on a smaller, quieter street, and then I cut the headlights and looked at the dark windows of houses, the blank faces of doors.

On the right was an enormous evergreen bush. I parked in its shadow and stopped and listened. All the chemicals were moving through me, up and down my arms and legs, into my fingers and toes. My head was like some highway interchange at the edge of a city at night. It was empty, then a car, a truck, a van, a cab, raced through so fast that I couldn't keep track. There were only traces of taillights.

I breathed slowly and shut the engine off, listened to the ticks and hums, and looked around. Beyond the bush there was a big Tudor house with some kind of metal sculpture on the front lawn, a three-car garage, trees, more lawn and bushes, everything.

The car door creaked open, and I closed it quiet as possible, and the air was humming, my head was sparks and zings, but silent somehow too.

There was almost a path through the evergreens, and inside the bushes everything smelled like wintergreen Lifesavers. Then I was on the lawn, in the pale moonlight. Crouched over, scuttling, moving fast as a cockroach, I crossed the lawn, went around to the left side of the house, then I was in shadow again.

There were more trees and bushes at the back and side of the property, and I made my way into them, maybe thirty feet behind the back corner of the house. It was like a small woods, with rhododendron and lilac, Japanese maple, oaks, whatever.

No one could have seen me in here. I squatted down.

Maybe it was forty, forty-five degrees, and probably three A.M. by then. The house was huge. It must have had six or seven bedrooms, five bathrooms, a den, a library, a pantry, a formal dining room.

Everything inside must have shined. Moonlight fell on deep carpets, the crystal, the leather chairs. Up the curving staircase, past the grand-father clock on the landing, there was an oak railing and a window seat. Then a master bedroom, a bed with a canopy.

I looked around, breathed the night air, waited.

I huddled in the trees and bushes, smelled the dead leaves, the earth, the pull of the moon. And in that house, in that bedroom, under those covers, someone beautiful was deep in the arms of sleep. Someone was dreaming. Someone was far far gone.

5.

THEY CAME TO him at night, in darkness, when the whole world was silent and whispering at the same time.

Hush, Gramma said.

Shh.

Don't say a word.

And he didn't. He was quiet as darkness. He heard wind outside the windows, and the floorboards creaked as Gramma moved from the door to his bed.

She crouched down and put her hand on his shoulder.

Little boy, she said. Little Jackie.

You sleeping? she wanted to know. You gone to dreamland?

I know about that, she said. I know about dreamland and where you go. I know what you see and think about. I know all of it.

There was silence for a while. There was more wind outside, and then just breathing and waiting.

He could feel her heat, and her breath was sour. Her breath was hamburger and onions and beer.

She moved her hand up and down on his arm. She sat on the side of the bed, and he tried not to slide down the mattress toward her. She was big as a wall and warm, and he tried not to slide.

At night, she said, the sun goes to sleep, and it's covered over with blankets, and some things go to sleep along with the sun. Good little girls and boys go to sleep, and God pulls blankets over them. But he's careful the blankets don't cover their faces.

Don't cover their noses and mouths, she whispered, and her hand pressed his nose and mouth for a second, then let go.

They could stop breathing, she said so soft that he wasn't sure if he had really heard her. They'd try to breathe, but the blankets might block out all the air. And because it was so dark, nobody would know they couldn't breathe.

That would be so sad, she said, and she sighed. He heard her breathe in, all the way to the bottom of her toes, then all the way out. So there was no air left inside of her.

She put her legs up on the bed, and leaned her back against the wall, and her arm was on his side.

Beautiful, beautiful boy, she said. And her hand was still on his arm and hip, and tapped his side with each word.

We were so happy the day you were born, she said. So so happy.

And we thanked God that you were with us and healthy, she said.

Then there was no sound for a very long time. There was just wind outside, and slow breathing, and his mother or father walked past in the hall. A toilet flushed, and water ran for a minute or two in the sink.

Far away a car went by, and something clanged a long way away, then there was just more silence.

He thought she had gone to sleep, and he thought maybe he had gone to sleep as well, because it felt like the middle of the night even though there was a crack of yellow light under the door.

After everything, she whispered, and then she was silent again, and he thought she was whispering in her sleep.

The door opened, and Dad looked in. He said, Mom, and she said, I'm sitting with Jackie, and he said, Oh, and the door closed. His footsteps went away.

She said sometimes she was happy and sometimes she was very sad. So sad that all she wanted to do was lie in bed all day and night, and keep the curtains closed, and never move for anything. Not to eat or walk or go to the bathroom even. Just sleep all the time, and wake up to cry a little bit and feel the heaviness over everything. Over the room and the sky outside. The heaviness on your arms and shoulders and legs.

She moved her hand up and down on his arm, and he was so heavy and light at the same time that he was floating on a cloud somewhere and he was drifting slowly underwater, and for a minute, maybe longer, her voice came from outside. Came from the other side of the room.

It must have been a dream, because then she smelled like shampoo and baby powder, and there was no sliver of light under the door anymore. And Mama, not Gramma, was sitting on the bed, and she said he must be tired because it was almost eleven o'clock, and the angels were sleeping in heaven and all the little birds were back in their nests, had gone home to their nests, and the mother birds were covering the baby birds with their warm feathers.

Are you warm enough, honey? she said, and she leaned close to his face and her breath was milky and warm and moist.

You need another blanket, honey? she asked, and kissed his forehead lightly.

He whispered, Mama, am I sleeping, Mama? and she said it was very very late.

You're sleeping, honey. You're off with the angels and the baby birds and all the beautiful little children in the world.

And then he was far away, and for a long time nobody came in or came near, and the bed was warm and all around him. He was four or five years old and he wore blue pajamas with patterns of horses, and he was somewhere far away.

Then it was quiet for a long time. Quiet and soft, and maybe there was rain falling somewhere.

Then that hand again. That wall of heat, and breath with chocolate and something like medicine or something to clean the bathroom, to clean out the toilet. Something to clean away all the germs.

You were sleeping, Gramma said. You were in dreamland.

She was whispering, but it was a loud whisper. Her voice was loose and careless and sloppy.

You think you're so cute, don't you? she said. You think you're a million dollars and your poo poo doesn't smell, and you're just about the best thing since they invented the wheel.

She leaned close to his face, and he heard ice cubes clinking the side of a glass.

Who told you that? she said. You tell me who told you a thing like that.

She sipped from her glass.

Ha ha, she said.

The wind was gone outside the windows. She leaned heavily against his side.

All the boys and girls, she said, her voice slopping over the words. They couldn't put Humpty Dumpty together again. So he just lay there on the sidewalk.

And Jack and Jill, stumbling down the side of the hill. Broke their crowns, she said, and don't you think that didn't hurt.

She leaned forward and scratched a place on her knee, on her ankle. She made another hill of the mattress and he tried not to slide.

Then it must have been snowing outside. A thousand and a million tiny feet were out there, pittering and pattering, only not the way rain went pitter and patter. This was cold and had more wind, and he could see when he peeked that there was ice on the window.

Gramma was gone. He didn't feel her leave, but the door was open a little bit, and it was very very late. All the good little boys and girls in the world were sound asleep and had gone to dreamland.

There were candy canes there and purple elephants. There were rainbows and music from harps and violins and angels too. Angels in white, with wings on their backs. They smiled and nodded at him. They were as nice as kittens.

Jackie, he heard. Jackie, and the radiator hissed as though it was angry and the night was a secret.

Gramma whispered that a secret was something you kept hidden. It was like something you kept in your pocket or in a corner of the closet or under the bed with the shoes and the dust. You must never tell a secret, she said, because then it would turn into something else. Would turn into garbage and poo poo all of a sudden. Then everyone would know all about it, and when you told the secret, it wouldn't be a secret. It would turn into something ugly like a lie.

Mama and Dad would listen, and the priest and nuns and the police, and they would see that he was lying. He was trying to tell an untruth, to hurt his Gramma who loved him very much.

Then he would have to stand there, in the bright light of day, and tell what he knew was really a secret. Only then it would be a lie. And it would smell so bad that they would have to hold their noses.

Mama and Dad would cry to hear it, and the nuns would blush. Then the priest and the policeman would grow very red and angry in the face.

Do you know that, Jackie? she asked, and leaned so close to his face that he couldn't breathe except to inhale what Gramma had breathed out.

I'm asking you, young man, she said, her voice a flat ruler.

He moved his head slowly up and down.

Because when I was a girl, she said, they took me away, and I didn't know where I was going, and I didn't know what I had done.

Do you understand that? she said, and he wanted to cover his ears because he knew she was going to tell a story and bring him to places where he didn't want to go.

Jackie, she said. Little boy, she hissed in his face.

Ice tapped the side of a glass, and the wind made the sides of the house sigh.

He moved his head up and down.

They took me in a car at first, she said.

Men in black coats. Men who had not shaved for many days. They had dark eyes and it was always night, Gramma said.

I never knew what had happened to Mom and Dad, and my brother and sister. Just that they were gone and I was in a car, and it was always night and always cold, and I had to go to the bathroom.

He tried to squeeze his ears shut, but she leaned over him, and put her fingers in his hair, brushing strands behind his ear.

The trees had no leaves on them, and there were hills and rocks, and there were always animals in the woods not far off, crying and howling. Lonely and hungry and cruel because their mothers wouldn't take care of them.

She whispered, We didn't know your mother, and we took her in. She came home with Bill, and we didn't ask any questions. She just walked in like it was any day of the week, and all we knew was that she was from the nuns and her mother and father left her, and she had nobody in the world.

Someone walked by in the hall, feet light as feathers. Gramma was quiet for a long time. Her hand was on the side of his head. The wind blew outside and he could picture snow swirling to the ground and blowing like powder on the grass and trees, on the clotheslines and fences. Snow would cover the whole world like a cold blanket. Snow would make everything whispery.

Then he was dreaming and he was in the woods, and the bare branches of trees were clicking overhead, were rubbing against each other, and moaning and sighing and clicking.

Her voice was a hiss and a sigh and she said she was very sad and very sorry. And lonely and she said there were so many things inside that couldn't get out. That could never come out even though she wanted desperately for them to come out.

She was so buried and frozen and stuck. And she wanted to speak, and there was so much to tell, only she couldn't even open her mouth to say them. Or she'd open her mouth, and no words would come, like some person with a dim bulb for a brain.

She said, I'm so sorry, Jackie, and her hand was on his shoulder and side. A sweet little boy like you.

She leaned close to his ear and whispered low. She said, The world is full of stories and lies, so many stories and lies and all of them are going at the same time. Singing and calling and saying and speaking, and then you hear only silence. And you can never tell what to believe or who to listen to.

She said, All the little girls and boys in the world are sleeping, and some of them are in dreamland, and they're under covers, and they have pillows under their heads.

But sometimes people come into their rooms at night and take them away to places anywhere in the world, or even to the planets and to other solar systems. Up where the moon and the stars are.

So you went to sleep, and you thought you were sleeping, and everything seemed like a dream. All kinds of new people and places and things. Some of them were scary and some of them were nice, but you could never tell if it was real or a dream, a story or a lie or a secret. And sometimes a story turned into a lie, or a secret became a story or a lie.

She said she was once a little girl just as he is a little boy.

I had blue eyes then, she said, and I liked to look out the window, and I liked to look at pictures in books and imagine I was in the picture, in a faraway place.

Then Mother got sick, and I had to go away and I didn't know where I was or if Mother had died or gone away forever.

I didn't mean to do any harm, she whispered, and he felt her tears fall on his arm like drops of rain in a field.

Everything was always dark, and water dripped at night. There were other boys and girls, and all of them had big eyes and very pale skin, but none of them could speak. They would try to speak, but the sounds that came out were only grunts and moans and sighs.

And I would go to sleep every night, she whispered, and pray that I'd wake up and everything would suddenly be different. I was anywhere but where I was.

6.

I'VE BEEN HERE all my life, too, just the way he had, only I live about five blocks from the house I grew up in, and almost never lived anywhere else. After high school I went to Mass. Bay Community College for two years, working nights and weekends at Newton-Wellesley Hospital, doing security. After that I transferred to Northeastern. Leslie and I got married right after I graduated, that July as a matter of fact, and we had an apartment near Newtonville Square that first year. On Madison, which is on your left coming from the Mass. Pike, the one with the sub shop on the corner.

Leslie's father died that year of a heart attack, the same month Tim was born, so she was at the wake holding a crying baby not three weeks old. But it wasn't so bad because you had your birth and your death right there in the viewing room at Conway Funeral Home. The beginning and the end, as Jesus said in the Bible, and one of them kind of helped with the other.

I was taking the tests for the fire department, and still working security, and it looked as though I'd be getting on the department that fall. And Etta, Leslie's mom, wanted to sell the house after John died, and move into the income apartment in the back part of the house, and we didn't even sleep on it for a night or two. We said yes right away. In October I started on the department, and we moved into Etta's, here on Crafts Street, in January, with Etta going to the apartment, of course, and by May, with Tim not even a year old yet, Leslie's got another bun in the oven. And that would be Kathy. Then two years after Kathy, Luke comes along. Meanwhile my mother and father are only five blocks away, two blocks down Crafts and three over on Linwood Avenue actually. And my little brother Kevin was still living there with them, going to Mass. Bay, and wanting to get on the department like me. And my sister Joan is working for the phone company and living with her boyfriend over to Brighton, waiting to save enough to get married.

I was surrounded, believe me. Plus once you're on with the fire or the police, it's like you've got all these brothers and uncles and nephews all around you. It's always out for beers, or over to someone's house for a ballgame on TV, or in-town for a Red Sox or Bruins game, or some kind of picnic, or someone's getting married, or having a baby shower, or somebody's mother or father or great-aunt dies and I'm putting on the blue suit and the dark tie and standing there. And no matter what it is, a wedding, a funeral, a baby being christened, and it's someone's brother's kid, or a cousin or something, you always end up feeling for them. Wishing them luck at a wedding or fighting the tears off at a funeral or feeling all happy inside at a baby—even when it's only the friend or cousin of someone you work with.

My mom and dad are still with us, and doing pretty good for their age. They're in their seventies now, and retired of course, and Kevin still lives with them, believe it or not. Thirty-eight years old now and still sleeping in the same bedroom he slept in thirty years ago.

He's on at the post office, just like Dad was, and I don't even like to ask when he's gonna settle down on his own. But he's there to shovel the walk and cut the grass and put the trash out Thursday nights, and that helps them. No doubt about it.

Dad has the heart, which he takes pills for, and Mom has arthritis, but they do okay, as I said. I worry about Dad still driving, and Mom is always doing too much. I'll come over and see her down on her hands and knees, scrubbing the floor, and I try to talk to her, tell her she's not twenty-five years old anymore. But what're you going to do? Both of them worked all their lives, since they were kids really, and you're not going to say to them, I'm sorry, you're sixty-five years old, you can't work anymore. I guess both of them will keep doing and doing till the day they die, God help them.

So I have my family all around me. Always have and always will. Once in a great while, after dinner or on a Saturday afternoon when I'm not working, I'll tell Leslie I'm going to the store or I'm stopping by to help someone move a couch or a refrigerator or something. And I'll get in the car and just drive. Always out past Newton, to the west. Past Wellesley and Wayland, to where the houses aren't packed so close together. I'll drive on those winding roads, and sometimes there are barns and a few houses out in a field, and the houses are set way back from the road and spread real far apart.

There will be lots of trees and some woods and ponds, and suddenly I'll notice how big the sky is, and maybe I'll notice a cloud or a bird moving across the sky. And I'll see a single house, alone on the side of a hill maybe, and I'll wonder who lives there, and what they do for a living and what they think about. Because you never really know, do you? You just can't tell.

And then I always think of John Connor, and what he did, and how strange it was to see him on television, with his jacket pulled over his face so they wouldn't take his picture. Because I knew him since the first or second grade at least. All the way through, I was in school with him, and I can tell about a thousand different stories of him standing at the edge of things, of the playground, and kids saying, Jackie, c'mon, wanting him to play, and him just standing there and not moving.

Or when we were in fifth grade at Carr School, George Kerr and Donald Ford and one or two others in the sixth grade picked him up in the boys' room, turned him upside down, and dunked his head in the toilet. He came into Miss Revessi's class, his hair dripping, and water running down his shirt and sweater, and Miss Revessi said, John Connor, what happened? And I remember to this day. He said real quiet, Nothing.

But she brought him out to the hall, and then to the principal's office, and eventually they got it out of him about the toilet.

Kerr's old man, who had a drinking problem anyway, had to come to school, and everyone heard sooner or later, and some kids called Jack Toilet Head even, and everyone laughed of course because that's how kids are.

And no matter what happened, he never seemed to say very much. He blinked his eyes and turned away, and sometimes kids threw snowballs at him, or pushed him into puddles, and then everyone would just laugh. Although most of the time kids just left him alone, they pretended he wasn't there.

Jack had brown hair, I remember, and blue eyes and he always had freckles. He also had this strange rubbery mouth that twitched and never seemed to smile. No matter what he did or where he was or what anyone was saying to him, he never knew how to respond.

My mother always had this thing about wounded birds. Take in every stray cat and dog and buy a chance or a box of candy or ribbon and wrapping paper from every single kid who knocks on the front door, trying to raise money for the Girl Scout troop or the class trip to Washington, D.C., or the heart or lung or kidney society. And somehow she knew about Jack and the Connors, probably from P.T.A. or just from talking to people in the neighborhood, and for a little while, back in about fourth or fifth grade, she was always after me to become friends with him.

So for a while I would ask him to come over to the house after school or on Saturday, or we went riding around on bikes, and two or three times I was over to his house—the big house over on Clifton that's still there and empty since everything happened. I'd only go in for ten or

42

fifteen minutes when he was changing into sneakers or telling his mother where he was going, and I remember this real strange feeling in there, and I don't think I'm saying this because of what later happened. There was this old-time feeling, like maybe nothing had changed in the house in fifty years. Everything felt kind of old and still and closed up, like they never opened the windows and nobody except the family—the parents and the grandparents—ever went in or out. Nobody ever came to visit the Connors, it seemed like, and the shades and curtains were mostly drawn, and the furniture and everything was real heavy and dark.

They lived up on the second floor, Jack and his mother and father, and one time the father was just sitting in the living room, like a statue or something. Not reading the newspaper or looking at TV or listening to music or anything, but sitting there like a statue in church.

And Jack didn't even seem to notice. We went down the hall and into his room, and I think he put on sneakers or a sweatshirt, and then we went down the hall and down the stairs and outside, and I remember how good it felt to be outside again, and kind of funny too. The way you feel after you walk out of a movie, and it's still afternoon and the sun seems bright and strange.

The only other thing I remember about that house from back then was when Jack couldn't find his mother upstairs, so I followed him down to the apartment on the first floor. And it was even darker than the second floor.

Jack's mother was talking to the grandmother, and I was standing in the doorway behind Jack, and while he was saying to his mother that he was going out to ride around or just over to my house, the grandmother looked at me, and she never said a word. And the way she looked is something I'll never forget. She just stared at me like I had done something terrible to her, by coming into the house or something, and she never nodded her head or said hello or how do you do or anything like that, and I remember wanting to get out of there as fast as I could.

Maybe they were having an argument, or maybe she had just heard some bad news. I later told my mother and she said you can never judge or pretend to know what goes on inside anybody else.

If you can't find something nice to say about someone, don't say anything at all. That's what Mom was always saying.

And even though I liked Jack Connor and thought it was okay to try to be friends with him the way Mom wanted me to be, after a while I just drifted along, and never much saw Jack except to sit with in the same classroom, or to say, Hey, Jack, in the hall or street or on the playground at recess.

Later, I guess, he never went to college even though he seemed real smart and I think he was reading books all the time. He worked a little at one job or another, and a few times I guess from what I've heard and seen in the papers, he moved away for a couple of months or went out to the state hospital at Medfield for a little while. Went to the mental ward there a few times.

Then on the radio and in the papers they were calling it the Death House and the Chamber of Horrors or some such thing—and now they're going to put him down like some sick cat or dog.

And most of the time, during all the years I knew him, he was just this pretty quiet kid who kept to himself and never bothered anybody, and probably that's why he got picked on. Called names and pushed around, and that's why Kerr and Ford, those bastards, did what they did to him. Put his head in the toilet.

Jack had no friends to stop them, to say, No, you can't do that, or even to run to tell a teacher. It's always easier to pick on someone who's small or weak or alone. I'm not proud of that either. That I stood there and watched kids spit on him or knock him down. Call him Faggot, Pussy, Fairy, Asshole.

I think about those things, the way kids would be to some other kids, and I want to cringe. I feel ashamed. Even though I was just a kid too. And I don't know, and none of us could know, what happened behind closed doors or what went on inside him or anybody, and what would happen all these years later. And not only to Jack Connor, but to kids all over the place.

And I think too of something that happened one day during this recess in junior high. It was spring and for some reason they left us out on the playground for a long time after lunch. We were in seventh grade, I remember, and seventh- and ninth-grade kids were outside together. And there was this pickup game of basketball going on. But it was kind of crazy—as much a football game as basketball, because there were at least ten kids on each side, and lots of shoving, and then someone tackled Gary Dickerson, who was in the seventh grade, and there was even more pushing.

Kevin White, who was this big ninth-grade kid, kept pushing Jack Connor around. He'd walk over and give him a hip check like in a hockey game, and then he'd shove Jack from behind even though Jack wasn't even near the ball.

It was weird because kids grow a lot during junior high, usually all of a sudden, and Kevin White had to be a foot taller and at least fifty pounds heavier than Jack. And Kevin was a really good pitcher on the baseball team. He wasn't generally a mean guy, a prick, but he was that day, at least to Jack.

After about the fifth shove, Jack was starting to cry, and then he called Kevin an asshole, and White said, What'd you call me? Jack said, Asshole, again, and Kevin punched him in the face. And Jack went crazy. He started groaning and making these strange animal sounds.

He got White on the ground, and he got behind him and had him around the neck, choking him. And about five kids had to pull Jack off him because I swear he was gonna choke White to death. If we hadn't seen it with our own eyes, nobody would have believed Jack had it in him. And I think kids who had given Jack a hard time in the past had to think again after that.

People never really picked on Jack Connor much from then on. He went back to being real quiet and standing at the back and side of things and never saying much.

I think of that sometimes now, when I take the car keys and kiss Leslie and say I'll be out a little while. Twenty or thirty miles west of Boston, on one of those country roads with the trees and the cows in fields, I'll look out at all the space and the emptiness. And I'll think of Jack Connor and what he did, and I'll want to hurry home to Leslie, and to the kids. To hug them. To say how much I need them, to say, Don't ever leave me.

Then

7.

I WAS THERE on the third floor a long time. I was there just about forever. The sun coming through the windows at a slant, then from higher up, and then late in the afternoon the light would soften, would turn yellow and gold, like something polished and old and valuable. Then the sky in the west would get cobalt blue, then electric blue, and would sometimes turn the color of sherbet, orange and raspberry.

And the clock always ticked and whirred, the second hand moving so slowly that I would watch it move minute after minute just to make sure it didn't stop. And all the while it was so quiet I could hear the air moving in and out of my nose and mouth, then all the way down to my lungs. And my heart going too. Thump and thump and thump. Forever and ever. Until the end of the world.

Then it was like floating in deep space. In the vast cold and darkness and silence. Just planets and stars. Past Jupiter and Saturn and Uranus.

47

Past Neptune, and finally, at long last, past Pluto, blue and solitary, at the edge of the solar system.

Late at night was always nice because the sun was gone, and the streetlights made small circles in the darkness, and the rest of outside was always shadows and a black blanket over the whole world. And sometimes I would shut out all the lights on the third floor and sit for hour after hour in a chair in the living room. My eyes open and fixed on a dark spot across the room. Then I'd try to hold my breath, and when a car passed out front, or when the toilet flushed downstairs, it was as though it came from the other side of life or the universe or something.

Dear God, I prayed. Dear God in heaven.

Dear Lord.

Holy Mary, Mother of God, pray for us sinners, now and at the hour of our death. Amen.

And all the heads in church as I remembered them were bowed down, and the strange, beautiful smell of incense, and the priest raised his arms, and I was thinking this, was remembering from a long time ago, how the words were in Latin, and Mom said Latin was an ancient and holy language.

Was crucified, died and was buried, the priest said. And on the third day, he rose again.

Valium was yellow when it was five milligrams a tablet. The ten-milligram Valiums were blue.

Dr. Chandler gave me a prescription for fifty Valiums, with four refills.

Dr. Chandler was thin and had short gray hair. His office was in a house near the hospital in Brighton.

Valium for the nerves, he said.

Fiorinal for headaches.

One hundred Fiorinals, with four refills.

And Dalmane for sleep. Thirty milligrams. Sixty capsules, with three refills.

Mom said this when I was little, and I remembered it. Why do you do this to me? Why do you do this?

She said, What is wrong with you? Are you sick or something?

She said, Once they get you in the dentist's chair, they do what they want with you. The needles and drills. Their sharp little blades.

You think they care? she said. You think they give a damn?

Money, she said. That's all they're interested in.

And don't you forget it. Don't even think for a minute.

Gramma's big hands moved slowly in the air in front of her face, and her teeth were perfect and even and white. They were not really her own teeth. I bought them at the grocery store, she said and laughed, and the welfare paid.

Don't you believe it for a minute, she said, and then she said, You watch out outside. You be real real careful.

They put poison in candy bars and just leave them there on the sidewalk. And some little kid, some greedy little kid comes along, and he says, Oh boy, isn't this my lucky day.

Gramma said her father never said an angry word in his life. Even when he was dying with the cancer, and the pain was so bad he wanted to scream out for God to take him.

Her glasses were like an aquarium. Her cloudy blue eyes swam.

And Dad crying. Dad saying he was so sorry.

Lying in bed, and Gramma saying, Get up, lazybones, or the gypsies will come along and take you.

He told this. Dad said, Come here, and he put his arm around my neck, and he said, They cut me up. They tried to hold me down and cut them off.

I fought, he said. I fought and screamed and thrashed.

We love you very much, Dad said, and his breath smelled like pine trees.

Then Mom said he was gone for a while. He wasn't feeling too good and he was gone to get some rest.

He gets tired, Mom said, and Gramma said that if Mom and that little bastard would just leave him alone, then this whole thing, and she stopped.

Gramma said, For the love of Christ.

Then I was gone for a while. I was nineteen or twenty years old, sometime along in there. I had driven in a car to get away. And I was in a room with a flapping window shade. And car horns and trucks and voices were outside and down below.

But this wasn't the hospital. There was no cage on the window, and nobody with a needle was coming in and rubbing a spot with a cold cotton ball on my upper arm. Nobody said, Up. Up. It's time to get up.

I drove a long time. Drank coffee and bought gas, and watched the white lines on the roads. Went past farms and hills, went through Albany and Akron.

And in the room I could sleep, and back in Newton they would realize I was gone and then they would be sorry.

She had dark hair and she sat down next to me and asked what I was drinking, and did I mind if she joined me. This was when I had stopped driving, and I was very tired.

She was Alice or Alex or Adela, and she lived nearby. She came here sometimes because she had to get out, and it wasn't the greatest, but it was okay.

You know what I mean? she said.

In the heat like this, she said.

Sometimes, she began, then she puffed on her cigarette and blew smoke toward the ceiling.

I don't know, she said.

Then we were in the room together, and we each took a Valium, one blue, one yellow.

What do we want with this? she said, and I said, With what?

She waved her hand at the window and at a water stain on the wall. With any of this, she said.

With you or me.

What do you want? she asked me, and she started to unbutton her blouse. You tell me, mister, what you want, will you please?

Mom said it was all one big mistake. One bad decision after another.

We didn't ask for you to come along, but God knows there you were, and all Bill would do was cry and worry about what his mother would say, and what in the name of God was I supposed to do then?

Her own mother had put her in an orphanage, and she couldn't even have been seven or eight, if she remembered correctly. Her father. My God, he was not much of anything either. Always with a drink in his hand when he did show up. Singing a song and always wanting her to sit on his knee and saying how much he loved her, and boo hoo hoo he was sorry she didn't love him the way he loved her.

Jesus Christ, Mom said. Jesus H. Christ on the cross.

The welfare lady said that some day, if I worked at a job, and showed up on time and was polite and cooperative, then I could have a nice car and maybe an apartment that wasn't on the third floor of my mother and father's house, and maybe I could even meet a nice girl sometime.

To go to the movies with, to have a nice dinner, to walk on the beach, and who knows what else, she said.

She turned over some papers on her desk and pushed her glasses higher up on the bridge of her nose.

Now there's something at a restaurant in Newtonville. A place that's looking for help. It's nothing very fancy or great, but it would give you a start and get you out of the house, she said.

Past Akron, on Route 18, I went through Medina, Ohio, and past farms and woods, and by then the sun had gone down. I was driving for a long time, to get away, and then I stopped for coffee at a diner somewhere near Norwalk, heading toward Toledo. I took a blue Valium and two Fiorinals, and the road was empty, and for a while there were woods on both sides of the road.

Then I saw her standing at the edge of the road and woods, a backpack at her feet, her thumb out.

She said, You're no sicko, are you? And she smiled.

I said I didn't think so. I was just a guy moving around.

She was from Bridgeport, Connecticut, and she had dropped out of U. Conn, and she had a friend in Madison. Was I going anywhere near there?

She said she'd be happy to drive all night, to do anything not to be standing alone in the dark, by all those woods and the sky as big as anything, and emptier than a dead person's eyes.

She said, You want to sleep, I'll drive as long as you want.

The engine of the car vibrated all night, and I scratched at spots on my arm and side, and she sang and hummed a song about her love being gone and why did he leave, and every half hour or so a truck went by and made the car tremble, then when it was past I'd feel the vibration of the engine again. Then I was sleeping, and a long time after that the car was parked at a rest stop and it was dawn and she was gone.

. . .

Grandpa smoked his pipe in the dark and when he sucked on it, the bowl turned red for a moment and made his face glow. This was before, I think. I was not too old. I was just a boy, but I remembered.

Cars went by on the street out front, and he watched their headlights and taillights, and he didn't move or say anything. Then it was dark, with puffs here and there, and a red glow for an instant, then more darkness.

In one of the true-crime books that I read on the third floor, it was sad because of how much the man loved the woman. He loved her more than he loved his life, and when she said she couldn't see him anymore, even though she still respected and admired him as much as ever, he thought something would explode inside. Something in his chest would rupture, or his head would crack open.

He just couldn't sit still. The pain. The torment of it. This was like nothing he'd ever known in his life.

One day she's calling him, she's sending him cards, and talking about all the things they'll do together. Camp out in the woods in Maine, go snorkeling in Florida or down on Cape Cod.

Then it's, Sorry, but my feelings have changed. And at first she talks to him on the phone, but then she's never there. So he shows up at her job, and the people she works with, they all look at him like he's got two heads or some disease.

And it's just that it hurts so much, hurts all the time. He can't sleep and he knows it's because of her parents. They don't like him. And if she'd only give him the chance to show her.

So he calls all the time, and sometimes he doesn't say anything. He listens, and hears, Hello, hello, then they hang up.

Next thing he's sitting in a parked car, across the street from her house. It's raining and raining, and he sits and sits. Just about forever.

The cops come, they ask what he's doing, but he's just sitting there. It's still a free country. There's nothing they can do.

So I'm walking on Center Street, above Newton Corner, and it's almost midnight, and spring. All these buds on the trees, pale green in the glow from the streetlights, and everything ready to explode in bloom.

All the houses are big. There are brick walls and trees, and I go left on Sargent Street, and cut down a driveway, along the side of a garage.

Over a fence, past trash barrels, a terrace, through more bushes. Lights are on in some houses, mostly on the second floors.

There's flickering light from television sets, and I'm right next to houses, standing right next to a house and I can feel its heat almost. Can feel the life inside there.

Over a chain-link fence, a dog barking somewhere. And there's some lawn furniture under some trees, in this big backyard.

So I sit down, and there's a woman in the kitchen. Dark hair, glasses, maybe forty years old. At a sink.

Up above, there's light in three windows, pulled shades.

The night is quiet, is getting deeper.

She said that they were not nice, those nuns in the orphanage. Mom said, You think you've got it bad. Ha.

Fat and stupid, she said. That's what they called her. And before that, in New York City during those years, during the Depression, that was no fun.

Cold water, a can of beans maybe. A damp mattress. The smell of piss and shit and old food.

You think I liked that? she asked.

She said, Ingrate. She said, I never saw, in all my life, such rotten, such selfish, such ungrateful behavior.

What's wrong with you? Dad said. Is there anything I can do?
You look okay to me.

Don't think you're the only one ever felt not so good in his life. You can always go back there. Go back to the crazy house. We can call, they could come in a minute, put you in their special jacket this time, and then you can't come back here anymore. No more, Welcome, mister.

You'll be history, and that's the end of that.

In one of the books I read on the third floor, he sat at the bar for a long time. Had a beer, took a pill, had another beer, another pill. Then he was easy inside, he could be anything by then, and he waited for the right one to come along. To say, Hi.

How you doing?

You look nice.

What's your name?

They were seventeen or nineteen or twenty-two. They had run away, or they lived at a friend's house, or they were staying at the Y.

They sold pints of blood. Worked at Manpower. Posed for pictures.

There was a friend named Freddy. A little brother somewhere.

A sister who got raped by her mom's boyfriend.

Fucking asshole, they said.

They liked gin or rum or vodka.

They liked dark beer, and weed, but only if it was really, really good. Otherwise they just fell asleep.

They were burnouts. Dopers. Fuckoffs. Freaks. White trash or black trash. They couldn't hardly read or add, or they were wicked good at math and loved that science fiction shit. Those monster fucking death rays and shit.

In a book they were in Cleveland. In San Jose.

In a book they had blond hair.

In a book this happened in Florida, on the Gulf Coast, or in Michigan, near Lansing.

There was a 7-Eleven, and it was open all night. The music was loud and they hadn't slept in three nights. It was warm out.

Nobody gave a shit.

55

He said, What's your name?
He said, What's up?
You okay? You wanna try some of this?
Don't be afraid, he said. And that was the end of that.

8.

I SLEEP FOR an hour or two at a time, and then stay awake a little, and then sleep some more. Most of my dreams are about flying high above the earth and looking down and seeing rivers and lakes, trees, hills and houses. Sometimes I swoop down low to get a closer look, and people are down there and they reach up their arms to snare me. Their arms seem to be made of rubber or long nylon string and their hands are like talons, and soon there are hundreds and hundreds of them, waving like fronds on the floor of the ocean, and I dart like a fish, trying to avoid them.

Or I dream of dark houses at night where water drips down walls and there are strange whispery sounds that seem to say, Jackie, Jackie, then there are sounds almost like words, but as I move through the halls, through the dripping rooms, I can't make out the words.

When I wake up I am here again, in this cell—which is six feet by eight feet, cinderblock and steel, all of it painted gray. I look at my hands and arms, my feet, my legs, my stomach and chest. When I look in the small metal mirror over the sink, I am always surprised to see myself, to see the big eyes, the thin lips, the heavy face staring back at me.

They come with the pills in tiny white cups, and I take them greedily like food or affection, and then I think at times that I can feel the chemicals spreading through my body, not only in my blood, but into my tissue and muscle, the nerve and tendon and bone.

The men never look at my eyes. They look at their own hands, or at my chest or stomach, or at the floor. They have stone faces, most of them. Chins that are gray and blue like iron, and glassy eyes. Even their hair is combed carefully back and held in place by a plastic sheen, and their movements are fast and stiff and mechanical. I listen for gears, for levers or clicks or tiny wheels moving, but I hear instead my own blood, and the chemicals moving into my toenails and into the follicles of hair on the back of my hands.

There is a clock on the wall in the hall, just across from the door, and its face is white, its hour and minute hands black, its second hand red. I have watched it sometimes for an hour or two, for as long as I can stay awake with the chemicals doing their work—the steady sweep of the red hand moving forever around and around like some blade cutting each strand of time, turning the future into the past, possibility into fact, *could* into *was*. The minute hand is more subtle, and far more slow, but I can see it too move as I watch, move in response to the second hand, come along behind like a punctuation mark, saying that yes, it's true, it's now past, and now will be over, will be done, will be history. And the hour, too, like a door, like a mile or foot or inch—all going in this circle, around and around, but somewhere else it's being recorded on what looks like a long straight line, going all the way back to when we lived in caves and had clubs and looked out over an icy expanse, seeing the steam we breathed into the world.

And such quiet, such dim hovering sounds that are so far away, but sometimes so close that I can never tell where the sounds come from, or if they are even there at all.

Father Curran said to pray. Said to say Our Fathers, and Hail Marys, and to say especially Acts of Contrition and to remember all the time I am praying that Jesus loves me and is waiting for me, and that everything will be right, will be pure, will be as one once again in some thing or place or time.

He is old and his face is yellow and red, and there are brown spots on the backs of his hands, and his hands shake when they pray and when he puts his hand on my arm. He wears a black shirt and the white collar in front, and a gray or brown cardigan sweater over everything.

Pray for forgiveness, he says, for the souls of the faithfully departed, for the sorrows of the night in the garden, when for a long long time Jesus prayed, and even in the darkest part of the night he knew that his Father in heaven would be with him.

When the lights go out, I close my eyes and imagine a sky above me. A black sky with a pale white moon and stars, and maybe wind moving in trees.

A time ago, at night, in summer maybe, in a place a long way from here, miles and years ago, the air was soft and smelled of pine, of lilac, of shampoo and sweat, and she said she was very very happy to be there like that.

She was Karen or Kirsten, and her skin was pale like the moon and seemed to glow, and she came from Colorado, from a house that had many rooms.

She said, We can lie here all night if we want to. You tell me everything you know about me. Where I come from and what I like and how I met you and where we're going to be next year.

She said, Can you do that? Or you want me to do that?

Her lips were soft, were cool and warm, were light on the spot above my eyes. Her breath was warm and smelled like toothpaste, like moist mint.

She said, You were walking in the mountains for a long time. You were climbing higher and higher because you wanted to see for as far as possible, wanted to see what was on the other side.

She slid her hand under my shirt, on the skin of my chest.

Am I right? she asked. Is that how it happened?

You were tired. You wanted to meet someone like me. You hadn't talked to someone in a long time.

She said, So I came along, walking on this path, just looking at flowers, picking up rocks and sticks, and then I saw this guy.

The silence seems to hum, to stretch out on all sides of me, and I feel the wall, and see dim light in the hall, down at the other end.

This is two or three in the morning and everything will be erased and that will be a good thing.

You are no good, I whisper.

You are ungrateful. You are ugly, you are stupid, you are selfish, you are cruel.

You are creepy, I whisper. Dirty, smelly, disgusting, greedy, lazy, dishonest, corrupt, weak.

God could not love you or want you or even hope for you.

If you sit in a dark place and clench all your muscles, and curl into yourself, then maybe you can disappear. You can become like an insect, although even an insect has a purpose and a place.

Maybe air, although air can be pure.

So lie still in this darkness and say I am wrong, I am guilty, I am lost, I am base.

Make me go away, make me stop, make me disappear.

Father Curran says, Lord, make me an instrument of thy peace. Where there is hatred, let me sow love.

His voice is so low I almost can't hear it. His eyes are yellow and blue, and he is so tired he can barely keep his eyes open.

The darkest place in the world would be a cave or a pit, on an island, a thousand miles from anyone or anywhere.

The smallest, loneliest place would be a room at the top of a house where the floors squeak and wind blows steadily against the windows, and there is blood moving through veins and where a heart is doing its old work.

He says that anybody can be redeemed, can enter into the love and grace of Jesus, and his hands shake, and his voice is low and faint.

The farthest, deepest place would be a room, would be dark, would be silent and cold, a place where nobody could leave, where someone could never be quiet ever again.

9.

THEY DANCED, AND he watched from a doorway near the corner of the living and dining rooms, and they danced around from the couch to the big chair to the dining room table, then back again, and all the time, on the radio, Frank Sinatra or Perry Como or Dean Martin sang, and the music was loud and filled the rooms. Gramma and Grandpa, Mom and Dad, they laughed and hummed and moved around, and sipped from their glasses, and Grandpa smoked a cigar, and kept it in his hand even as he held on to Gramma, one hand at her waist, the hand with the burning cigar at her shoulder.

He was supposed to be sleeping. He was supposed to be all the way up on the third floor in his new room there. But he had woken up, and had gone down to the second floor and there was just water dripping in the kitchen sink, and the light on over the dining room table, and plates and glasses still sitting from dinner. And downstairs, he could hear the music. When he got to the hall downstairs in back, he could feel the cold from outside.

There were doors to the cellar, to outside, and to Gramma and Grandpa's, and all the noise and light and heat was coming from under Gramma and Grandpa's door.

He knocked softly, but nobody heard, then he knocked again, and after a third time, he opened the door and went in, and went quietly to the inside hall.

All the lights were on, and the music was loud. The floors seemed to rattle and shake with the movement, and then he saw them dancing. Moving the way he had never seen them move, their eyes shining, and their movements quick and easy and graceful. And the radio singing about love, about everything taking wing and going far away on a cloud.

Then Dad saw him in the doorway by the hall. He stopped, and Mom stopped, and after a minute or two Gramma and Grandpa stopped. The music kept going, kept singing about love and hearts and the face of love turning to gold. Their faces were shining and there were drops of sweat on their foreheads and the sides of their necks.

Grandpa said, What're you doing?

He couldn't open his mouth.

They kept looking at him.

The song on the radio ended and another song, a much slower, sadder song, came on.

Dad said, You couldn't sleep, and his voice was slow and loose.

Then Gramma reached down and said, Poor baby, couldn't sleep. She opened her arms, and he went to her. She patted his back and said, I know, I know.

She was warm, and she said, Okay, honey, and he could see Mom and Dad's shoes, and the bottom of a chair.

Gramma stood up and said, I'll take him up, and Mom said, No, I'll, and Gramma said, Go on.

So the music was playing, and Grandpa sat down in his chair and puffed his cigar, and Mom and Dad began to dance slowly around again.

I never knew, the song went. I never cared so much.

And then you, it went, and then the night was blue again.

Gramma held his hand, and they went down the inside hall and through the kitchen, then into the back hall.

Gramma closed the kitchen door and she sat down, in the darkness, on the steps. She set him on her lap, and put her arms around him, and pressed the side of her face to the side of his face.

Oh, Jackie, she whispered. Jackie, Jackie, Jackie.

She sat for a long time, and the music was still playing, and he could feel the cold air from the outside door.

You couldn't sleep? she asked, and he didn't say anything.

She nuzzled his neck with her nose.

He shook his head slowly.

Why not? she asked. Bad dreams? Scary dreams?

He nodded.

Monsters and goblins, she whispered. Things with red eyes.

He could see her smile in the dark. He could feel her breath as she talked.

You think about what's in the closet? she asked. What's under the bed or in a corner?

She patted his shoulder.

I know, she whispered. I know, I know, I know.

She shifted their weight, and leaned her side against the wall.

I was a little girl once, she said.

That's hard to believe, isn't it? she said. An old lady like me. Gray hair, bent over like a crone.

She was quiet. The music kept playing, and he heard his mother's laugh, then his father's voice saying something low.

So you got up and looked around, and everything was dark, she said. And you thought you'd get up, maybe sneak around in the dark, maybe go spying around.

See what they're up to, she whispered. See if anything's going on around here. Things that happen while you sleep.

She tightened her arms around him, and rocked back and forth.

Sneaky, sneaky little boy, she said. Quiet as an Indian. Doesn't think anyone will see him or find out.

But we saw you, didn't we, honey. We saw you there in the hallway, all wide-eyed and innocent.

She whispered, That's okay, Jackie. That's all right, honey. You don't have to say a thing.

She patted his back, his shoulder, the back of his head.

Did you think about the cellar when you were sneaking down here? she said. Did you think of what's down there late at night?

The door's right there, honey.

Maybe you want to go down and sneak around in the dark. Creep around like some quiet little Indian, and see who you can spy on.

He shook his head, and she said, I don't know about you sometimes.

Sometimes I think that you need to learn a lesson or two. Need to be taught to mind what people say to you.

She set him on the stair, and stood up. She snapped back the bolt from the lock on the cellar door, then opened it. He could smell the musty air. The dust and moisture.

Come here, she said.

He stood up, and she put her hand at the back of his head.

The stairs down were dark and smelled of mold.

You see down there, she said.

He nodded.

Next time you can't sleep, and you think you might want to go sneaking around, you remember what this looks like. You think you can do that for me? You think you can remember?

She squatted down, her face so close to his that he couldn't see her.

Because I love you very very much, she said, I try to look out for you, and do what's best.

You know what I mean? You can feel that, can't you?

She put her hand on her chest.

You can feel what's in my heart, can't you? she said.

Because my weak son, my Bill, he went out and he defied me, Gramma said.

64

He got up and went out and because he is so weak and so pitiful, he defied me. And your mother, who comes from no one and nobody, she sees how weak he is, and she preys on that.

So what can I do after that? she said. I try to love her and I try to love you. And I see you sneaking around, and I know that you're not much different than your mother.

So go down there, Gramma said, and tell me what you find while you're sneaking around.

She pushed him down a step or two, then she closed and locked the door.

Everything was almost completely black, and he could feel his heart thumping and he had to remember to breathe. The sound of the music was farther away, and as he went slowly down, the stairs creaked and the musty smell grew stronger. If he didn't go all the way down, Gramma would know, and make him go.

At the bottom of the stairs he saw the big, hunched shape of the furnace, and he sat on the concrete floor. He leaned his back against the bottom stair, and saw faint gray light from two windows high on the cellar wall.

He thought of spiders and bats, and he thought of creatures with red eyes and leathery wings, creatures that had tentacles and bristly hair on their arms and legs. He curled up and clenched his body and made small whimpering sounds, but the spiders, the things with wings and many legs and bulging eyes—they wouldn't go away.

Then he heard a faint whispery sound near his ears. It sounded not like wings or sucking lips or padded feet, but like something soft and low.

The voice went, Waa waa waa waa, very quickly and very low and he listened carefully.

Okay, little boy, it said. Then there was a second whispering voice saying, Little boy, little boy, and a third voice, even lower and fainter, saying, Jack, Jack.

Sweet little boy, a voice whispered. Sweet little brown-haired boy. Blue-eyed boy.

Another voice whispered, Boy with freckles, boy with dreams.

Then it seemed like there were even more voices, each lower and softer and quieter than the first. There were four and five and six voices. And each one knew him, and each one whispered soft breath in his ears.

Don't worry, one said, and then lower still, another said, Little boy, this will be all right. Nothing will hurt you here. Nothing will harm you.

Then for a second there was a single deep voice, a woman's voice, but someone who was not as old as his grandmother, and she said, We know about this, little boy. We see this and we know about this.

Then the high, soft voices came back, and said, We see them all the time, and it is not right.

Not right, not right, a voice echoed.

We will get them, a new voice said, a man's quiet voice. For each and every time.

Little boy, the high, soft voices said, and each voice was a soft string, and each one began to weave in and around the other strings of sound, whispering at his ear.

We see, they said, and, All the time.

He put his hand on his cheek, at his ear, but felt nothing. Just his ear and his hair.

He said, Our Father, who art in heaven, hallowed be thy name.

But the voices didn't go away. They got softer and quieter, and he lay down on the concrete floor, his head against the side of the bottom stair.

The dim light in the high windows got farther away and fainter, and he must have been dreaming. He was outside, very late at night, and someone was carrying him in their arms. Grandpa was carrying him, and then he was in Gramma and Grandpa's bedroom, and Mom and Dad were standing in the doorway, and Grandpa was sitting on the bed next to him, holding his head up, and Gramma was standing next to a bureau pouring something from a brown bottle into a small paper cup.

This will make you feel all better, young man, Gramma said, and Mom laughed, and Grandpa said, Not too much, Belle.

It was yellow liquid that smelled like medicine and like something for cleaning the floor.

The light in the room was dim, and Mom and Dad were smiling at him, and Grandpa was saying, There you go now, sport. There you go.

Gramma held the cup to his lips, and he coughed, and she said, Okay now, and Grandpa said, There, there. In a dream maybe. In something he might have read or remembered.

Mom and Dad were standing behind Gramma and Grandpa, and their faces were long like the faces of horses, then round like the moon or a balloon. The ceiling seemed close.

He sipped a little from the cup and gagged, and felt it burning down his throat. Then Gramma gave him water to sip, then he sipped more from the cup of medicine.

The bureaus in the room were very tall and made of dark wood that was polished so much that they held the light.

There was deep organ music, and Dad said, This ought to do him, and then Dad laughed in a wavery voice.

This will show him, Mom said, and her voice was from somewhere outside the room, and then he sipped more from the cup.

His head was heavy as a rock, and his eyelids were weighted, and his arms and legs couldn't move.

Grandpa was whispering that everyone had to learn sooner or later, and that it might as well be while you're young and more likely to remember.

Dad and Grandpa were dressed in red and Gramma was dressed in black and Mom was in white. The ceiling went slowly, and even though his eyes were closed, he could see them.

It was later still and all the lights were out, and he was lying in a room, and there were candles flickering in the room, and strange airy music—like heaven had opened, whispery and far away, then much closer. People in red and black robes stood around, and they said things in a language he didn't understand.

They said, Hisogoth and Barnuncle and Shewithin, and other voices chanted quietly.

When he opened his eyes and looked up, there were faces staring down at him from the darkness high above. They wore hats with sickle moons and stars, and most of the faces were very very old.

One face smiled, and then a soft, low voice by his ear said, Jackie, Jackie, and more quiet voices said, They won't hurt you, they won't hurt you.

We love you, the voices whispered.

Gramma held his chin up and said, A little bit more, and she pressed the rim of the cup to his lips.

Grandpa whispered that when he was a boy, it snowed for three days in a row, and the snow was higher than the windows, and then Mom was in New York City, and there were huge boats floating on the East River, at night, in the fog.

10.

IT SEEMS THAT most people in the funeral business are born into it, or perhaps they marry into it, although once in a very great while I will hear of an individual who is simply interested in the work or somehow compelled to work for a mortuary, and who will then go on to embalming school. Upon graduation they (or he or she, as the case may be) will find a position with an established business, and with luck and perseverence, they may go on to buy an existing business, or in a rare case, they will build their own business from the ground up, so to speak.

For me, of course, it was a matter of my father already being established in the business in Newton Corner, as his father, Merton Conway, was in the business before him. Old Merton was a tall, thin man with a long face and very dark eyes, I seem to recollect. From what I have ascertained from discussions with my own father, Maurice Conway Sr., Merton began in the business here in Newton Corner with a certain Mr. Henry, sometime in the 1920s, because Merton needed a position and because Mr. Henry needed a young, willing fellow with a strong back and steady nerves. Someone, I gather, to help pick up the deceased from the hospital or home, to help carry the coffin, to hold doors, and assist with the bereaved members of the families, such as they might be. The duties, as one might imagine, were, and still remain, myriad.

Over time, Merton took on added responsibility, and eventually, sometime in the 1930s, during the Great Depression, as luck would have it, he went to embalming school and then became certified by the state board, such as it existed in that era.

To make a long story somewhat shorter, Mr. Henry got along in years, and my grandfather bought the establishment from him in 1947, two years after the end of the Second World War. My father took over the Conway Funeral Home from his father, and I in turn have largely taken over the home from my father. Although, as anyone familiar with small, family-owned businesses will readily inform you, the process of succession is anything but a smooth and easy road. It involves a long apprenticeship, son to father, novice to master, so to speak, and years of a gentle push and pull that can fluster and frustrate even the most fore-bearing individuals. The older generation does not want to let go, and the younger generation is certain that it is long since past the ripe time. After the financial arrangements have been worked out and agreed upon (for this is—notwithstanding kinship—still the formal sale of a business enterprise), the father maintains a reduced financial interest, and good-ness knows, an even more heightened personal interest.

So the father, who has sold the business, is now getting on in years. But he is still quite healthy and alert, and perhaps he has more time on his hands. He notices that the son has had new carpeting or curtains installed in the viewing rooms; the son has invested funeral home funds (a great deal of those funds, the father will assert) into a computer system on which the son will be able to efficiently record the business records. The payroll, the outgoing and incoming flow of monies, inventory, cus-tomer payment schedules. But the son has bought a larger and more complex computer system than he strictly required, the father implies.

And so forth and so on. But over time, and with an artful display of tact and understanding and patience on both sides (something that this industry is noted for), the situation can be managed successfully. In short, I kept Father involved in the business. When there was more than one funeral occurring at the same time, I enlisted his assistance. I listened patiently to his advice, but made clear to him that I would sometimes follow it, and sometimes I would not.

As the years passed, two years, four years, six years—and then heaven forbid, an entire decade and more, and Father saw that not only did I not run the business into the ground, as he had feared, but that the home flourished under my leadership, he became more relaxed. In time, he even began to laud some of my innovations. That, of course, makes each of us pleased, and gives us peace of mind.

And peace of mind, if you will excuse the rather clumsy transition, is exactly the service we provide to our customers. And our customers, as I point out repeatedly, to our employees, to neighbors, to friends, are not the deceased but the living. To put it in the most base and perhaps crass terms, the deceased do not pay our bills. The deceased do not care in the least.

Our business, I have long felt, and Father shared this sense as well, is perhaps the most widely misunderstood business in existence. People often make jokes about it, people will rarely know what to say when you meet them in a social setting, and they casually ask what the nature of your work is. I respond that I am in business, and if they pursue the matter by inquiring of me what kind of business, I will tell them that I own and operate a funeral home.

The responses of many, when they receive this information, would be amusing were it not so sad. Many will say, Oh, I see, and will then look away from me. One woman, a young gal in her early thirties, I would guess, once responded by saying, How strange.

It is rare, very rare indeed, for someone to say, How interesting, or to express any curiosity whatsoever. And Lord knows, people have never, in a social situation, said to me, That is an important and much-misunderstood profession. I am glad you are there to perform the service.

The individuals who do understand and who do appreciate our work, who value it very highly indeed, as a matter of fact, are those who are in most need of it. Which is to say, the families—the husband, the wife, the son or daughter, the brother, sister, grandchild, niece, father, mother, grandparent, aunt, or uncle of the deceased. They count on us in what are surely the most difficult and painful days of their lives—when a loved one has passed on.

These family members come to us in shock, in anger, some still unbelieving, numb with grief and agony. Sometimes, more times than I would have suspected in my younger years, they come to us with a feeling of peace, and perhaps of relief as well. They sometimes come to us with what seems like an almost superhuman calm and resignation in the face of what must be unbearable loss. I am thinking here, primarily, of parents who have lost young children, to accident or illness. Seeing a parent, a young mother, for example, who comes into the viewing room to see her five-year-old child in a coffin—seeing that mother as she looks at her daughter, as she strokes her hair or her cheek with a tenderness that is beyond words, then I know that what I do, the work and skill and the dedication I bring to my work, is not only valuable, but at some moments even, perhaps, a little bit noble.

When I say that it often saddens rather than amuses me to see how many react to a person in my profession—with incredulity, with revulsion, with fear—it is because of how human beings, particularly human beings in our society, view death. They perceive it not as something that each of us will undergo at the end of each of our lives, as a natural and perhaps fitting accompaniment to life—the dance of death at the end of the music of a life, as someone so aptly stated the matter once—but instead they see death as something unnatural and ghoulish, as a horror movie which each of us must view and enter into at the end of the long night of life.

It is sad, and at times it is perhaps tragic, but death almost never seems to me to be an unnatural event, or to be something from a horror movie. Only once, in my near twenty years in the business, have I encountered a death, or in this case deaths, that seemed to be beyond the pale, if you will. They seemed so dark and troubling to me, and to many individuals, of course, that I didn't know what to say or think. I could only move ahead and do what I have been trained to do.

I am speaking, needless to say, of the deaths of the three Connors in late August 1988. The grandmother, Isabel, and the unfortunate parents of that unfortunate man, William and Joan. The younger man, John, has been very much in the news of late, both on broadcast news—radio and television—and in the newspapers as well. He is scheduled to die, if you will, on May 12, only three weeks from now. The carnival atmosphere surrounding his pending execution is every bit as troubling as the murders themselves, and as troubling too as John's trial and sentencing.

But I am getting a little bit ahead of myself, I'm sorry to say. The emotions are stirred up, and I don't think as clearly and logically as I normally would. So I will begin at the beginning, as it were, and I will try to be brief.

The family first became known to me when the grandfather, Edward I believe his name was, passed on in August 1973. He was an eighty-two-year-old man who died of a pulmonary embolism, and the wife of the deceased, Isabel, and their son, William, came to me to make arrangements. They seemed like quiet, modest people. They wanted only one evening of visiting hours, followed by a funeral Mass at Our Lady's Church, followed by interment at Newton Cemetery. They picked out a coffin and made a deposit. At the time, I was struck by how few visitors there were. In all, perhaps a dozen at most in the two evening hours. The church was nearly empty at the Mass. This was my first year in the business and I think this lack of mourners struck me as somehow sad.

They paid their bill on time, and that was all that I heard of them.

Then fifteen years passed, and the second deaths in the family were as loud and garish as the first death was quiet. It was a Sunday morning, I remember, and there was a news item on the radio—three family members were apparently killed by another family member in Newton. The thirty-four-year-old son was being held without bail. For the next few days the headlines fairly shouted the news about Death House, as they dubbed it, and The Monster in the Attic.

Dr. Caines in the Coroner's Office first called us about handling the funerals. Someone had found a record which indicated that we had buried the elder Mr. Connor, and Dr. Caines asked if we would handle these funerals. We wanted to get these poor people embalmed and into the ground with the least amount of fuss.

So I enlisted the help of my father, and I asked David Harper, from the Harper's Funeral Home in Newton Center, to assist us. I have no wish to go into the details of the matter, except to say that we did the best we could under these highly unusual circumstances. There were no other family members aside from the son, who was being held for the murders of the deceased. There had been an elderly sister of William, but she had passed on the previous year. So there was nobody to consult except for Dr. Caines, and the police and several functionaries of the state welfare office.

David Harper and I had to visit the house on Clifton Street, with a police detective as an escort, to get clothes in which to bury the Connors. And on that day, which was still unbearably hot, as it had been for that entire summer, we went to the house, which had been displayed so widely on the news. There were reporters and television cameramen, not only from local news organizations, but from national news organizations as well, and they tried to accost us for comments and questions. I must admit now that I thought of them at the time as vultures, and as parasites on the body of horror. Though I recognize now that they were merely performing their duty.

Walking inside, in those small and ill-lit rooms, seemed very confining and uncomfortable to me. Because of what had occurred there, only a few days previous. I could not help but imagine, and I would guess that with David Harper the same would be true, what it was like to be a ninety-year-old woman, or a parent who was in his or her late sixties, and to have the hulking figure of John Connor stalking, late at night, overhead, or down these very halls and in these very rooms. This was not my role or my function, not in any way, shape, or form, but I do not think I would have been truly human if I did not have any of these thoughts.

At one point, I was on the second floor, in the bedroom of William and Joan, while David Harper and the police detective were downstairs on the first floor. I was looking through dresser drawers, in search of stockings and such, and I happened to spy a small oval picture frame, not much bigger than a half-dollar coin. In that frame was a photograph of William and Joan and John, and John, I would guess, was perhaps seven or eight years old, and it seemed as though the photograph was taken outside on a sunny day, perhaps in their own backyard there on Clifton Street. The first thing that struck me about the photo was that all three of them were smiling and looked for all the world quite happy. And the second thing that struck me was that the photograph was in a dresser drawer, almost hidden from view, and not displayed on top of the dresser as you would expect to find in many homes.

But to be brief, and not to dwell on anything for too long, we held a wake for the three, because we thought it was the right thing to do, and the wake was mobbed by hundreds, and I dare say, thousands of people. The police had to come to keep people orderly and in line. As you may expect, the newspapers and television stations were there, and people from all sections of Newton and Greater Boston were there. Individuals came from Maine and Vermont, and from as far away as Texas and Missouri. There were wreaths and floral tributes, and on both the local and national news there was film showing the Mass at Our Lady's Church, with the three coffins side by side in front of the altar railing. The scene at Newton Cemetery was quite similar. Throngs of mourners, many of them sobbing as though they had lost their own mother or father or grandmother.

I could not understand it, and my father said he had never seen its like in nearly a half century in the funeral business. In the *Boston Globe*, a headline stated, "A City Mourns."

There were profiles of each of the decedents, and even longer profiles of John Connor. "What Went Wrong?" the headlines asked, and "Could Authorities Have Known?"

What they did not know and could not have reported was that John Connor came to the funeral home very late on Tuesday night, near midnight. The Mass and burial would occur on Wednesday morning. The doctors at Bridgewater State Hospital, where John was held for observation, felt John should be able to pay his last respects, strange as that phrase may sound.

So sometime after eleven-thirty, I would guess, he arrived, under heavy guard, handcuffed, with chains and shackles on his legs, and heavily sedated as well, I surmise.

I let them in: John Connor, five or six state policemen and detectives, and several hospital officials. John went to each coffin—they were all open—and knelt briefly, and seemed to pray. Then they led him out into the night and its attendant darkness.

Now they have asked me to perform this final service for the Connor family and I have agreed. John Connor himself apparently requested that I be solicited for one final act, one last turn of duty, and I have agreed, as I said, as I feel I must.

An autopsy will be performed on him, as it was performed on both his parents and on his grandmother—as state law requires in cases of what it calls unnatural death. Following the autopsy, John Connor's remains will be delivered here in an unmarked van. I'm to prepare and casket the body, and a Father Curran will say a brief Mass here at the home. Then the Newton Cemetery will open the grave there on the hillside where his parents and grandparents lie.

We will do this in secret, even in the dark of night if necessary. We will bury him with the dignity that he seems to have so lacked in life. At that point, my work with the unfortunate Connor family will be over.

Then

11.

THE DOCTOR SAID, Who are you? What do you do with your time?

He had blond hair, combed carefully into place.

Do you have any disturbing thoughts? Any thoughts that in any way upset you? he asked.

When it's night, he said, and you lie down in bed and maybe you can't fall asleep, what do you think about?

How do you feel about living in your mother and father's house? At your age?

Do you masturbate? Do you think about sex?

About women without clothes on? Or men without clothes?

Little girls or little boys?

Do you ever hear voices in your head, asking questions or telling you to do things?

Do you feel any unusual urges, to do or say things that you wouldn't normally do?

Do you drink?

Watch television? Read books? Have any friends?

Any ringing in your ears? Spots or blotches in your field of vision? Night sweats? Blackouts?

Have you ever come to or woken up as though out of a dream and found yourself in a place you've never seen or with people you've never met, and the people seem to know you?

In a book I read on the third floor, his name was Charles, or his name was Richard or Earl or Duane. His name was Roy or Randy or Cliff.

He lived in a suburb of Chicago, and he visited sick kids on the children's ward of the hospital, dressed up in a clown suit. The kids had cancer or heart disease or bad kidneys. They were bald from chemotherapy. They had dark rings around their eyes, or gray skin, or weak smiles and no energy to laugh.

Hi ho, he said, and he laughed, and he handed out balloons and lollipops. His shoes were enormous, and if you squeezed his red nose, it made a funny beep sound.

His name was John there, and at home he had handcuffs, and he knew a trick. You put the handcuffs on your wrists, hands behind your back, and without the key, if you twisted the right way, one wrist forward, the other wrist back, you might get free without using a key.

There were drawings and paintings of clowns, hanging on the walls of his living room and den. Clowns with painted, funny faces, with teardrops painted on. Clowns that were always jolly and happy, but always sad and lonely inside too. Inside, where it was impossible to see, unless you looked really carefully and closely. How trapped they were inside. How they couldn't get out. Those awful feelings.

I said, Yes, and, No, and, I think so.

I said I would try very hard.

I said, I know. I understand. I see.

Yes, I said. Absolutely. Of course. No problem.

I smiled. I blinked my eyes, crossed and uncrossed my legs, folded my hands in my lap.

I hadn't thought of it that way, I said. But now that you mention it.

Now that I think of it, I said.

Randy, in a book, liked to drive at night, out into the desert, or up into the hills above the city. From a park up above the city, at night, there were a thousand winking lights, yellow and white, and shining with promises and whispers.

His sister, when he was little, used to hug him and say how much she loved him. But then his mother and his stepfather came back, and then he and his sister had to sit up straight or else, and clean their plates, if they knew what was good for them.

They called their stepfather Neil, and he had a crewcut and muddy boots all the time, and he always had a cigarette going, the smoke curling up in front of his nose and eyes and hair.

Some nights he'd just sit and smoke and sip from a bottle or a can half the night.

There was a man in there, in the hospital, who had stabbed his father, and he had nicotine stains on his index and middle fingers. He wore glasses and never said anything.

There was a woman who walked slowly up and down the corridors, hour after hour, all day, and all through the night too, and she never said anything either.

The social worker said that Mom and Dad had not wanted to call the police, but I was so thin, and I had stopped taking showers. All you have to do is get a treatment plan and take your meds and follow the ward rules, and then when the thirty days are up, the pink paper, the commitment paper, expires, and the hospital won't petition a judge for another one.

A fisherman found a body, floating face down in a marsh. The body was partly decomposed, and was clothed only with socks and a bracelet around one wrist.

A man walking his dog early in the morning found a body.

Two Boy Scouts on a camping trip found one.

A hiker. A jogger. A husband and wife taking their toddler daughter for a stroller ride.

In weeds. Staring blankly at the sky.

An arm akimbo. A leg twisted weirdly around.

In a book the man in St. Louis cruised the streets along the river, First and Second Streets, Lewis, Memorial Drive. He parked and climbed over an embankment, and squatted near the train tracks. He saw lights winding on the other side of the river, in Illinois, and he wondered what time it was, what month, what day of the week. He wondered how long he would drive.

This was in a book, and cars went by out front on Clifton Street.

The man in St. Louis stood by the side of the river a long time. He thought it might be May, although it could have changed to June already. He'd been gone a long time.

I turned a page, and adjusted the shade on the lamp, and looked at a crack on the wall over the window in the bedroom.

I lit a cigarette, sipped, turned a page. The clock said 3:27, and it was dark outside, at the edge of the curtain.

In Philadelphia there might be rain, there might be a breeze blowing in from the west. In Baltimore the streets were mostly empty. The streetlights were shining on the tops of parked cars. Cats were moving in shadows, raccoons were nuzzling trash barrels and Dumpsters.

. . .

The doors and windows were all locked and the windows had bars on the outside. The walls and floors and ceiling were long and shiny, and went on forever. Went around corners and down other halls, and past clocks on the walls that were behind cages so that nobody could tamper with time. Sounds whispered and echoed, and someone rubbed a spot on my upper arm with cold cotton, then stabbed with a needle, and my head was under water or under glass, and people moved their mouths like fish in water, and no sounds came out. Just bubbles of air.

There were more whispers, but they came from a light socket, or from a dark spot in the wall.

Now we have you, they said. Now we know where you are.

Don't try that, they whispered, the air sibilant with the rush of air.

Don't even think of doing that, they hissed.

The telephone did not ring and there was no sound downstairs because all of them were asleep. The walls were quiet and the ceiling was quiet, and I could stay as long as I wanted to, provided I was quiet and careful and paid my rent on time and took my medications.

We don't want you to come back here anymore, the woman said, and it's not because we don't like you. She laughed. She said, You take care now, and she stood up and patted my arm, just above the elbow.

And so the third floor was quiet and careful, and at three or four in the morning, in the quietest, deadest time of night, nothing moved or whispered or breathed, and I would never do anything that would make me go back there.

I would watch the wall, and I would hear a truck on the Massachusetts Turnpike, maybe a mile away. And do other things too, things that would promote adjustment and well-being.

Wash the dishes.

Eat vegetables.

Keep the apartment neat and clean.

Shave.

Shower.

Go to church and pray.

Make an effort to get out and meet people.

Exercise.

Keep regular hours.

The woman in the office folded her hands on her lap and smiled at me. She said it sounded like things were going okay.

Who knows, she said. Maybe, eventually, sometime in the future, you could meet a special someone.

She had one client who went from the hospital to a group home to a supervised apartment all in one year.

He was doing great, she said. He was really happy, and if he kept it up, held on to his job and saw his therapist regularly, he'd be back in an apartment of his own any day now.

He always felt the pressure, in the book. Felt like he had a tight metal band around his head, and Alma was always telling him to go out and get a job and stop complaining. So after a while, after only a year with her, he left and got a room of his own.

A bureau, a closet, a chair with the plastic on the seat part ripped. And a radio playing down the hall all the time. Guitars squealing and singers whining and the ads for cars and pimple medicine and movies about people trying to kill other people.

They take everything from you, bit by bit by bit.

Your dignity and your freedom and your pride.

Get the fuck out, they said, and don't let me see you here again.

Next time, they said, you make the team. Next time, you take a ride with us, and it'll be ten days or thirty days.

Mom said, You think you've got it so tough? You think nobody ever had a hard time except you?

No one ever gave me anything, she said. Except for a hard time and a slap in the face.

You wanna hear about a hard time, she said. Ha.

I could tell you a thing or two.

Her hair was thin and white and I could see the shape of her skull in the light.

There were boxes and papers piled on the dining room table. There were newspapers stacked on the floor. There was a container of plant food on a table near the window. Glass cleaner, a radio that didn't work, a portable vacuum cleaner. There was a comb and a brush and a pair of pants on a chair.

The light fixture overhead had extension cords running from it, taped to the ceiling with gray duct tape. A television and light and portable tape player were plugged into one end of an extension cord.

My mother coughed blood and worked on her hands and knees and she was grateful to have the work.

New York City, she said. Ha.

People selling pencils, selling apples.

Wearing signs around their necks that said, HUNGRY. NEED WORK. WILL DO ANYTHING.

I know, she said. Don't you tell me. And don't think you can't go back to the bin again. One phone call to the cops is all it takes.

The dishes piled in on a conveyor belt, on trays, and I took off the silverware, separated the cups and bowls and dishes and glasses, and stabbed them in big green trays for the machine.

The room had yellow tile on the walls and ceiling, and smelled of garbage.

Walter worked the dishwashing machine. He slid the green tray in, pulled down the door, hit the button.

Walter lived in a group home and had been working in the dish room eight years.

Belle said things on television scared the hell out of her and she thought about them often, especially at night. When she woke up and couldn't sleep, and all she wanted was a little peace and a little quiet, and did I think that was too much to ask? For God's sake.

She sat in her rocking chair, her big hands in her lap, knitting. The needles went click click click, and the television was on, but the sound was low.

She looked at me and said, Why don't you make something of yourself?

Jack. Jack.

Why don't you do something?

We tried and your mother and father tried, and you just sit there and sneak around like some cat or wild animal or something. Like you're hunting or stalking.

Like a ghost that won't rest because it can't.

You're not a ghost, Jack, she said. Even if you think you are.

She pulled more yarn from the hank that was in a bag at her feet.

Your father used to sleep all the time too, she said. All day and half the night.

Some nights I'd wake up at one or two in the morning, and he'd be standing there at the foot of the bed, staring and smiling. And I'd feel my heart go, My God.

I was scared to say anything, and his father was out like a baby, practically, and I'd say, Bill, what is it? What in the name of God?

Then I had locks put on the doors, and around then you came, and who knows what else.

But just standing there, at the foot of the bed, that weird little smile on his face. I get shivers now, just thinking about it.

12.

SUCH A QUIET boy. Such large blue eyes. So many freckles on his nose and under his eyes and on his cheeks.

A thin line of a mouth, and standing as straight and still as a board, for hour after hour if he had to.

Because he was learning a lesson. He might not like it, but some day he would be thankful. He would look back and wish that he could thank them. That they had been there to teach him a thing or two, but he was an ingrate.

By then, by the time he was old enough to be thankful for the lesson, it would be too late. They would be dead.

Then he would be sorry. Standing at each of their funerals, while they were lying, cold and still and dead, in their boxes. And nothing left to say. And then at the graveyard, the priest saying, Rest in peace, and, Go with God, and, Make this bed, this permanent, final bed, with awe.

The hole in the ground and men standing around with shovels, waiting to push clumps of dirt on top of the coffin.

Gramma would be in there.

Or Grandpa, or Dad, or Mom. Her hands folded patiently, wrapped in rosary beads, on her stomach.

Too late. Too late. Too late for thanks or I'm sorry or if I'd only known.

So if he didn't like the cellar or the closet or standing outside the back door at night, on the porch, and hearing them lock the door on him, then he'd have to learn.

One time Gramma took him to walk in the woods, after they drove ten or twenty miles in the car, and the trees were everywhere, and the branches and leaves so thick overhead that sunlight was almost green and thin.

Gramma said she loved being in the woods, where everything was clean and pure, just the way God wanted it. The way he intended it before Adam and Eve ate of the tree of knowledge and were banished.

Out here there was wind and sun and rain. There were birds and squirrels. Eating nuts and berries, going about their business the way God intended it. And when God looked down from heaven and saw the little animals, it made his heart glad.

They walked on a path in the woods, past trees and rocks, and the birds sang. They went up a small hill and around a bend, and there were no people or roads or cars for many many miles. Gramma said God wanted it to be like that. That is how he intended the world to be. But people came along in their greed. They fornicated and they had children they were not intended to have. They had ugly and black thoughts that stained the purity and whiteness of their souls. The souls God had given them to keep as white and pure as the new-fallen snow.

They came to a small clearing in the woods, the size of a room, and Gramma knelt down in front of a large gray rock that was partly covered with moss.

We need to pray, Gramma said. We need to ask his forgiveness.

Hail Mary, she said, over and over. She said ten Acts of Contrition and the Lord's Prayer and the Twenty-third Psalm.

They knelt for a long time, and overhead the sun continued to shine thinly down.

Finally Gramma stood up slowly and sat on the rock. She told him to keep kneeling. She said he had a great deal of forgiveness to ask. It was unusual to see such black stains on a soul so young.

His knees hurt and his back hurt, and he shifted his weight from one knee to the other.

Stop that, she said, her voice suddenly thunder.

You.

You, she said, and her voice shook, it was so loud.

She was silent and he wanted to stand up, wanted to move. Squirrels and birds moved overhead, and he heard the breeze make the branches and leaves whisk softly.

Nobody would know, she whispered. Nobody would have any idea at all.

She was quiet for a long time.

Something chittered in the distance.

I know what you think, she said. I know how you feel about me, but that only proves your corruption, your moral decay.

She stood up and stepped toward him and stopped. He felt her presence just behind him and to the side.

A knife, she said. A heavy rock. A piece of lead pipe. A short length of rope.

Then you would not grow into the monster you are surely becoming.

Because I try and I try.

I pray to God.

She said, I want you to stay here. It will be dark in an hour or two, and I will go off and wait near the car.

Maybe I'll get in the car, and get something to eat. Maybe some cake and some hot tea.

I need to think about this, and to ask the Lord for guidance.

And I want you to stay here. I want you to pray and ask God's forgiveness for the things you think and do.

Then she was gone, and after a while longer he sat down in the leaves.

The sun was at the side of the sky and the light was orange and gold.

He thought he heard branches snapping and twigs breaking. He thought he heard wings beating the air somewhere above him.

Then he was cold, and he lay down on the leaves. They smelled moist and thick. They smelled almost like the cellar.

He heard a flutter near his ear. He heard the shush of breath.

Then it was dark and a branch was snapping and Gramma whispered that he must be very cold and tired and probably hungry too.

She lifted him to her shoulder and gave him a cracker. She said that she had begun to worry about him. Out here in the dark with just his prayers and faith to protect him.

He was in the car, and she gave him a sandwich and a small carton of milk.

It's important that you know how much I love you and that God loves you, Gramma said. And God is a stern and demanding Father.

The greater the hardship, the greater the reward. Here on earth and in heaven. Ever after, she said. Now and at the hour of our death.

For death would surely come. To each and every one of us.

They drove in the darkness, and Gramma said when they got home she'd make him something nice and hot to drink, and then he could take a hot bath and get into bed and sleep till morning. He wasn't to say anything about the woods because that was their secret. That was between him and Gramma and God in heaven.

When they got home, he went upstairs to the second floor and all the lights were on, and seemed very bright. Mom was sitting at the kitchen table crying, the tears falling silently down her cheeks.

The table and sink were full of dirty dishes, and Dad was in the living room, wearing a white T-shirt and boxer shorts, sitting on the couch, sipping clear liquid from a Flintstones juice glass.

Dad said, Where you been? And Jack said, With Gramma.

C'mere, he said, and Jack went to the couch and sat next to his father.

You love your old man? Dad said, and he put his arm around Jack's shoulders and pulled Jack to him.

His dad smelled like sweat and mint and tobacco.

You love your old dad? he said.

Jack looked at his eyes, then looked away. Dad's eyes were intent and blurry at the same time.

Your old man loves you, he said, whether you know it or not. Whether you give a good goddamn.

Dad said, It's not easy, being your old man, you know.

Then he said, We love you very much. You know that, don't you?

Up to bed then, Dad said, and I don't want to hear a peep out of you.

He kissed Jack on the forehead, and his chin was like sandpaper. He squeezed Jack's arm.

Sleep tight, honey, Dad said.

The stairs creaked and the hallway on the third floor was dark except for a square of moonlight that came through the window and made a blotch on the floor.

Then he was in bed, and he must have been sleeping. Because then he heard shouting downstairs. Dad's voice and Mom's voice, and even louder, Gramma's voice too.

Don't you dare, Gramma said, and Mom said, I never, in all my life, and Dad said, Goddamn it to hell, and Mom said, You think for even a minute, and Gramma said, Who do you think, and Dad said, You shut your mouth before I shut it for you.

And then someone was sobbing, Mom or Gramma, and Dad was saying, I give up, I can't do this anymore, and Gramma, her voice lower, said, You just hush, and there was more crying.

He sat up, and there were movements at his ear and around his head. Small movements, strands brushing his ear and cheek.

Whispering, Hail Mary, full of grace, and he knew he should pray some more, should pray the way the strands of sound prayed.

He got out of bed, and crawled under the bed. He pushed his sneakers out of the way, and felt some dust on the wood floor. The metal springs were only a few inches above his face, and he pulled the bedspread down on the side of the bed so that he was completely hidden.

He said five Hail Marys, five Acts of Contrition, and five Lord's Prayers. He could hear voices downstairs, but they were quieter now, and lower and softer. They were like faint vibrations coming through the wood of the floor.

There were other vibrations, other strands of sound, whispering very softly at his ears. Saying, Jackie, honey, little boy.

There were cars passing on the street out front, every minute or two or three. But they were from some other dimension, some different space or time.

The whispering said not to worry, said everything was okay if he would pray very hard to God and to his only begotten son, Jesus Christ.

Then he lay still for what seemed like a very long time. The voices down below were quiet now and the whispering had stopped, and no cars passed out front for a long time. For five minutes, or an hour, or maybe for a day—though everything stayed dark and silent and that much time could not have passed.

Then there were footsteps on the stairs, coming up, and walking slowly down the long hall.

Little boy, Gramma said. Little Jackie, honey.

Gramma came into the room, and she sat on the bed.

She said, I know you're under there and I know you're scared and I'm very sorry for that.

You're just a little boy, she said, and this must not seem fair to you.

The voices at his ears whispered very quickly and very softly, and they seemed to be saying, JackJackJack, so fast that each word ran into the other and became part of it, so that they were all one long word, one breath in his ears.

Gramma said, None of us meant for anything to be like this. No matter what we say and how we act, we didn't mean for this to be.

She paused, and he heard her breathe in and out.

She said, My father had a beard and blue eyes, and he always wore a suit on Sundays. A wool suit that was gray, and that hung in the closet of his bedroom all week. Then on Saturday night, he took the suit out, and he brushed the suit carefully, and then he took a bath, and he sang songs while he was in the bathtub.

Do you understand that, Jack? she said. Do you understand what I'm telling you here?

The whispering in his ear was almost silent. It could have been the sound of blood flowing through veins and into capillaries. It could have been specks of dust settling on the windowsill, flowers or leaves unfolding in the moonlight.

He brushed his suit, and he took a bath, and he sang because of everything that was in his heart, she said. And on Sunday morning he went to church, and we could see it in his eyes and in his face—the happiness he felt, the goodness and kindness.

And he never said a harsh word in all his life, Gramma said. He never raised his voice, or felt a trace of bitterness or jealousy or rancor, in all the years I knew him, and that's what I'm trying to tell you. To let you know how good he was, how kind and gentle.

Gramma was quiet for a little while. She shifted her weight and the springs of the bed touched his shoulder for a moment.

My mother was different, Gramma said. She was very different from my father. She had those eyes, and I don't mean to speak ill of the dead, but her eyes just blazed like the fires of hell, and God forbid if she saw you, if she caught you and laid those eyes of hers on you.

God help the little girl or boy who happened to be nearby when she had one of her spells, Gramma said, and then she was quiet.

But my father, he was so tall and handsome in his suit, standing there in church, working hard all week, and then taking his bath and singing, and then standing there in church, Gramma said.

And none of this, this house and your father and mother, and you— none of this was supposed to happen this way—this late, and you under there and me here. None of it. And how everything is now. But we didn't know, and I need you to know that. How everything. How all of it.

13.

WHAT? I KNEW him what? Maybe—I don't know—maybe ten years ago even—out on R2, the acute-care ward at Medfield—and he was probably, I would guess, say twenty or thirty or so, though maybe a little older, maybe a little younger.

Who can say? Who's to know for sure?

Maybe Helen Cohen. She would know. She was case administrator out there then. She would know how old and what. Where he was going to and whatnot.

She would always say to me, Listen, Spider—and I would always listen to Helen Cohen. She had been around the track a time or two and she was a straight shooter, and I guess that she must have worked there on the ward ten or twenty or even thirty years, if that is possible. She had the gray hair, like my mom would say, to prove it. To prove how hard and how long and how much she worried all those years and times.

You're telling me a thing or two.

But Helen Cohen, she had the nice gray hair, cut short, so it looked pretty good, pretty sexy for a gray-haired lady, if I do say so.

Excuse me, please. Who said that word? Who said *sexy*?

Spider—that's me—did Spider say that?

Maybe, maybe not. Who can ever tell or know for sure?

So Helen Cohen, Mrs. Cohen, because she had a husband once, but I think he did get taken away to the beyond by the cancer. But she was still Mrs., I do believe, even though she always said, You call me Helen, and I'll call you Spider, you don't mind.

You just slow down, Spider, I say to myself, and try to concentrate on the thing at hand. Keep your eye on the ball. Bear down. Focus and concentrate when that ball, it leaves the pitcher's hand and comes in to Spider at the plate, fast as a rocket, but if Spider looks real careful, and keeps his eye on the ball, then pretty soon he can see it like everything's in slow motion and he can pick up the seams in the ball, the red stitches that hold it together, just the way former Boston Red Sox great Ted Williams, perhaps the single greatest hitter in the entire history of the game, the way Ted Williams could see the ball coming in.

Teddy Baseball. The Kid. The Splendid Splinter.

Boy oh boy.

You take your greats and your near-greats over the years—go back as far as you want—and he was one of the gods, on a very high pinnacle, no doubt about that. By God.

No harm, no foul.

So where were we?

The ball, it's coming slowly in, spinning slowly, and I can see a stitch, a stitch, and then, what, ten years ago, and John Connor, sure, I knew John Connor, although we called him Jack. I think everyone there on R2, we called him Jack, just like President Kennedy. He was John F. Kennedy on his birth certificate and driver's license, but his friends, they all called him Jack. And it was exactly the same with Jack Connor.

Ten years ago. And I knew him there on R2, both times he was in, because I was having quite a few of my own problems back then.

Dr. Sterne, he was trying to get my meds right. First Haldol and then Mellaril and Prolixin and a little lithium, then mix in a spot of Elavil or some such thing and maybe some Cogentin for tardive dyskenesia, and you had the complete chemical cocktail. All the time I go, Spider goes, way far up or way far down to the bottom of the basement, and sometimes things are talking to me, saying, Henry, calling me my real name Henry rather than Spider, which is how everyone knows me.

Voices say, Pick up that knife, Henry, and walk in front of that car or step out the window there on the fourth floor and see if the knife, the car, that fourth-floor drop—you see what that will do. That knife, why it's made of smoke or rubber, and that car, why that will go right through you because now you're smoke like the knife, and you won't fall to the ground either, you drop from up there.

C'mon, Henry, and the whole time I can tell that it's just some voice trying to trick me. But when everything else is going on—that sadness and not being able to get out of bed or take a shower or eat—you say, Why not? Let's give it a try sometime.

And hour after hour, for a long time, that's how all of that felt, and I spent so much time there on R2, or at Metropolitan State, or once in a while when the beds were full and Medicaid would let me, on the psychiatric ward at Newton-Wellesley Hospital or Waltham Hospital, or once over at Mt. Auburn Hospital in Cambridge, right near the Charles River. People running along the path by the river. Go by walking hand in hand, walking a dog, riding a bicycle. The boys and girls from Harvard and M.I.T. and B.U., why they go by in the boats, the members of the crew. They row and row, going by on the brown water down below. The sun, it was always shining up in the sky, and the leaves in the tree on fire.

My Lord.

Now here at 92 Kerr Street, for I guess almost four years now, I have just about everything I need. Share the room with Charlie.

He's a nice guy. Maybe he should take more showers and clean up around here a little better. But I like Charlie.

Spider goes to his day program on the blue bus, when it stops out front at 8:20 sharp every morning during the week. And if he's not up and ready, hair combed and teeth brushed and wearing clean socks and underwear, well then, too bad for Spider or Charlie or Jenny or anyone isn't ready. They will just have to stay home instead and miss all the fun and their friends at day program. Have to stay at home and mope around 92 Kerr with a long face, from dawn to dusk, and who wants to do that?

The first time it was on the news about Jack Connor, oh my God, on Sunday afternoon, I think there was baseball on. We were in the living room—this was at Hope House, way before Phoenix House and 92 Kerr—and Trevor and Manny and I think Kathleen, not Katherine, were there—they broke in and had a spot news thingy, and said, In Newton, three people were dead. The mother, the grandmother, and father, and the son—that would be Jack—was being held, and who in the world, and why would anybody, and what did that or anything mean?

They didn't have alcohol or drug rehab back then. You had the addicts and alkies in there with the crazies all mixed together. Because it was all the same thing. Your life all turned around and upside down and you had to come in there to the hospital, or else God knows what would happen.

Chris and Doug and Laura—they all had to kill themselves, and probably there were many more I can't remember.

Jack was very quiet all the time is how I remember him. Watched television and smoked cigarettes and walked up and down the halls some. Maybe said hello and hi and maybe hey once in a while.

Sat so quiet like a chair. Looking in front of him at nothing. The smoke curling up and Jack did not blink. Did not turn his head or either eye to see when Spider went by. When anyone went by in front of Jack. His face a mask and a statue. Pale stone and plaster.

He was pretty tall, I think, but pretty skinny too, not like the picture on television where he gained weight, and just looked like someone far away from anything.

You see that look. Raymond, who lived at Hope House, always had that look on his face before he went back in the hospital again. Last I heard, he had a girlfriend and a job, so you never know.

They always called me Spider since I was a kid because I was so long and thin, all arms and legs, and I moved quick just the way I talk quick too. I never minded at all. I think Jack, when he was in those two times, I think he must have called me Spider too. Even though—what—he didn't call anybody much of anything, he was so heavy and slow and sad and trapped inside himself like that. Peeping out from behind his eyelids, and from behind the hair hanging down his forehead and covering his eyes.

They were blue eyes, with shiny black circles right in the middle of the blue like a pool you could dive into. Spider, he would go right up to Jack. And he was just as tall as me, and skinny as string too—Spider and Jack. Only Jack Connor, he had wide shoulders, and those thick hands and muscles in his wrists and forearms. Veins popping out on the hands and arms. Skinny man buried under ten quilts of sadness, but you could tell—strong as anything too. Those hands and arms, they could take a hammer and pound rocks or haul sand or wood.

Whatever you want, Spider, I say to myself and anybody who would care to listen. All the staff on R2.

I stood there, right in front of Jack Connor. He's hiding down below his eyelids, behind this curtain of hair too. Peeking out like you're gonna shoot him, hit him, stick needles in his arms or hands or belly.

I said, Hey, Jack, you want a smoke? You want a handshake? A pat on the back?

Seldom is heard a discouraging word, and the skies are not cloudy all day.

Spider said that to Jack Connor all those years ago. And he looked out, and he said real soft like a whisper, Sure, you got a smoke, and I gave it to him, plus my smoke that's already going so he can light up his own.

No matches, no lighters, no nothing out there on R2. Shoelaces, belts, sharp objects of any kind.

Self-injurious behavior.

No sir.

So Jack. What. He takes a smoke, and he walks around, and never says boo barely to anyone.

They dry him out from the booze and the pills, and still, he is under the blankets. That depression.

Oh my.

That does weigh heavy on the mind and soul. On the shoulders, the neck, all over everything.

You want to hear, you talk to Spider.

So he never says much. They don't come to visit that I know. No Mom nor Dad nor Gramma that I can tell of. No old, bent-over, gray heads. Wearing long black clothes just hanging down on them. None of that.

I give him a smoke, a pat on the back. Next day, a smoke, a, Hey, Jack, how's it going for you?

Wave, a nod, a wink of the eye.

Say. Jack. You have your chin up, the wind at your back. Fair weather and following seas, my friend.

Maybe he's in there two weeks, three weeks, the full thirty days. They go to court, his mom, his dad, his gramma, they get some judge, he says, You're in for thirty days. A pink paper.

Homicide and suicide precautions. Maybe he took a swing when the mom and dad, when they call the cops to come take Jack to the hospital. Jack takes a swing at the cop, the nurse or doctor at the emergency room.

Jack. Maybe he stayed in that room all the time. At home. Just drinking, smoking his cigarettes, taking one form of medication or another.

Then a phone call, then cops, a swing, thirty days. You swing on anyone here in this hospital—why, we have a padded room, we have restraints, we have shots we can give you in your butt, your hip.

You maybe wanna go to Bridgewater State Hospital for the Criminally Insane? You think you might like that, tough guy? You be with the baby killers. With those people like to dig up bodies over to the cemetery and maybe take home some body part to cuddle and kiss and fuck.

You think maybe you would like to go there?

They light fires to get an erection. They like little boys or girls. They like to dress up different and hurt small animals just for the fun of it. Hear them cry.

So Jack and Spider and all the rest of us on R2, we move soft and speak soft and when they say, Jump, we ask them, How high? And when and how long?

Then you blink your eye, Spider, you scuttle down the hall when the voices come on and whisper, Henry, you want to try something new? Stay close to the wall and the corners.

Put your fingers in your ears.

Hum a song.

Say, Our Father who art in heaven, twenty, thirty times.

You blink your eye, and Jack Connor is finally gone home, and Spider thinks that is the last we see of him. Like most of the people in the world. You see them on the street, walking down the hall in the ward.

People here at 92 Kerr. Bob and Brian, my good friends. Stewart. Why, I know them like they are Spider's family.

Then blink your eye. One night you go to sleep. You pull the cover up, you think sweet thoughts, sad thoughts, safe thoughts for the darkness to console that part of yourself. You got a pillow, a comforter, Charlie already breathing deep and long like a train chugging.

You wake up and they're gone somewhere. Moved to California. To Costa Rica. To St. Paul, Minnesota. You live in their life a while, you care all about them, then you wake up in the morning and they're *G* for gone.

Many happy returns, and you don't even want to think of it or you'll cry and cry.

You say, They were so good to me.

You think, Boy, I did care for them.

How they smiled. They said to you one day—when Spider wants to hide under a rock, he is so low—they said, Hey, Spider. They put their hand on your shoulder, maybe for a minute or two.

Maybe walk up and down the halls there in R2. Walk outside, around and around Phoenix House. Maybe out in the woods.

Not even saying too much.

Just, Hey.

Have a nice glass of water. A cup of tea.

Sit on the steps out front at 92 Kerr. The sun, maybe it was shining on your face, five, maybe ten minutes.

Then they have moved on to some other place.

And Jack Connor did. Then later, maybe two years, Spider can hardly keep track, Jack is back on R2, and that time he was not as skinny, but still hiding down behind the hoods on his eyelids, the hair like a shade.

That time, that second time, well they got my meds adjusted. I think Stelazine, maybe some Desyrel for the sadness.

Spider will make those pharmaceutical companies happy.

You got some money, you put it in drug stock and Spider will make you rich.

Then you can sail a boat in the Bahamas, you feel the sun on your face.

So the second time, Jack was still standing at the window maybe, there in the dayroom on R2, and Spider—he was the one to leave. This time to Hope House and a stable life.

Years and years go by. People come, then they go along. The sun rises, it sets. Snow, rain, wind, hail.

And one day, Jack maybe hears a voice telling him to do it. Something has put on the terrible pressure. This awful, this powerful urge.

Now pretty soon, what. They will take him. Look him in the eye. The warden will read a paper. Some minister, some rabbi, maybe some priest.

Say, From dust to dust, and shed thy blood, and blessed be thee, and whatnot.

Wish him peace and calm and forgiveness.

Strap him in. Strap him down. Some last, some sad and awful goodbye.

Spider, what. Maybe that was eight or ten or twelve years ago. Out on R2. Jack Connor, he was standing, he was hiding behind, behind what? Behind everything. From what?

I don't know.

Blue eyes. Veins on the back of his hands.

He did something terrible. He stood, and lifted his hands, and he did not stop himself. And pretty soon. Someone else. Press a button, move a lever.

Then you have—what? You tell me. You tell Spider.

Then

14.

THERE WAS SOMETHING about the way they came to the third floor, came slowly up the steps, and one of them had a walkie-talkie in his hand. It went squawk and rumble, and the stairs creaked.

They wore dark blue uniforms, and there were three of them. Big men. One with sunglasses. With belts and guns, handcuffs, keys, pens, notebooks, and big arms and hands. They smelled of leather and smoke and aftershave lotion. They smelled like outdoors.

They said, Your mother and father called because they've been worried about you. You haven't been eating, and you didn't want to go to the hospital on your own.

They thought we could help. That we could take you somewhere safe, where you could get the help you need.

.   .   .

The doctor said, Name the last three presidents of the United States.

He said, What day is this?

He said, Where are you?

Do you know why you're here?

Have you been eating? Drinking? Taking any drugs?

All of it was quiet, was fever and dreams. People wavering and floating, and there was a me in there, and there was another me standing and watching. Still another, and another, and another.

A skinny young man with long brown hair, and a small boy with a few freckles on his nose.

People crouching, smiling, trying to sing or talk, swing a baseball bat, plant a tree, read a book.

I had been there a long time and I had just arrived, and if they would only give me my bottles of pills and let me go back to the third floor, I would leave everyone alone, and they would learn to leave me alone.

Then it was later, and I was back there, on the third floor, and everything was quiet.

I stayed in bed, closed my eyes, and listened very carefully.

Slower and slower, and a car went by, and the walls hummed, and when I opened my eyes again, I was in the middle room on the third floor, and everything about the police and the hospital, they had really happened—but some time earlier, and they had happened to me, but to a younger, different me.

I could figure it out if I went really really slowly, and if I barely breathed. Some part of my brain was still clear, and it would know all the whats and wheres and hows and whens.

Then I pulled the blankets higher and stayed quiet, and I was floating again.

.   .   .

They didn't know that I had keys to their apartments, but I did. When they went out shopping or to church, I would go down there, and listen with my ear next to the wood of the door, and I listened carefully as a cat.

Then I opened the door on the second floor, and the light from windows was falling in and lying, tired and weak, on the floors and part of the walls.

They had things piled all over everything. Clothes and books, newspapers and envelopes and magazines. Little cards with Jesus and his halo on them. Hair curlers and cups of dusty pennies. Empty bottles of wine and juice glasses that held stamped-out cigarette butts.

Down the long hall was a chair and a window, and out the window was the front porch and the tree in front.

I looked at the cracked ceiling, and up above, I thought, just a foot or so over the cracks, was my life, pressing down all day and night, and all the time, and I wondered how that felt for them.

On his small desk in the back room, Dad had rosary beads and books about the strength of prayer and the twelve steps to a higher power and understanding.

He said he couldn't sleep very well at night and he woke up sometimes, sweating and gasping for breath. That's when he would try to pray and try to meditate and make the bad thoughts go away.

Worry about losing his memory, or about losing the house or getting cancer, or his mother getting sick and dying.

It was hard, he said, to lie there in the dark, and not to have these terrible things race through your mind like fire trucks on their way to a fire.

Sometimes he got up to check the pilot light on the stove. He thought he could smell gas or he thought he smelled smoke. A few times he checked the furnace in the cellar.

.   .   .

When I went away, to the west and the south, and I drove all night sometimes, I thought of them when I passed towns and cities, and miles and miles of houses and barns and sheds and buildings. I passed tens of thousands of telephone poles with wires strung from pole to pole. I went past other roads and streets and highways, past canals and paths and darkened windows, and swingsets sitting, unused, behind houses or schools, and I might be in some town in east Tennessee or northwest Georgia, and there were more houses and parked cars, with car seats for babies in the backseat, and I would picture them in Newton, late at night, lying in bed.

Early one morning, at three or four A.M., I pulled off the road near Red Wing, Minnesota, at the bank of the Mississippi River. It was dark, of course, and I had to walk over an embankment of weeds, and through some bushes, and then I stood on a rise, overlooking the river.

And it was wider than a dozen highways and moving slowly past in the dark. And the surface of the river was full of the sky—of a three-quarter moon and stars and a few balls of cloud.

I was in Minnesota, on the west side of the river, with half a continent between me and them. And I hadn't taken pills in three or four days, and hadn't had any alcohol in that time, and I suddenly had the feeling that I could go anywhere and be anything. Walk away from Newton and the three of them, and go into a river or sky of possibility.

Then I imagined them in their beds, and I imagined myself standing in the doorway, watching them sleep.

The woman in Greensburg, Pennsylvania, was named Susan, and she said this was kind of amazing, seeing me in the park there, and starting to talk. Saying this and that. Your name, my name. Where you're from. What you're doing.

And making dinner, in the ground-floor apartment, in the kitchen of a house on a leafy street. There, somewhere in western Pennsylvania, not too far from Pittsburgh.

Susan with brown hair, and working at the library—how many years was it—and once upon a time, back in the late seventies, she was even married. For six years. Then she left him, and he didn't deserve it. She knew that now.

Forty-seven years old and living in an apartment.

Cutting onions and carrots. Washing lettuce. Turning the flame down low under the pot on the stove.

Just pasta with pesto if that was okay.

This is crazy, she said. I've never done something like this.

I said, I haven't either. I had brown hair and blue eyes and I was twenty-something years old. She could have been my mother, but she looked younger.

Her hair pulled back in a ponytail with red ribbon. Wearing black pumps, a gray skirt, a red sweater. Earrings were silver stars.

Said, Here, and handed me a glass of wine that was deep red, and in the kitchen we touched glasses and she said, Here's to you, and here's to good luck and passing through.

And she was soft, she was kind. Small gestures. Grated cheese, the way she pushed back strands of hair from her face as she smiled. She touched several fingers to the back of my hand.

Said, It's okay. Really, it's okay.

Said I could stay on the couch.

Said, For God's sake. Why not. Laughed. Put her fingers to my face.

Was shy. Susan was shy. Was soft. Smelled like flowers. Was so smooth. Was kind.

Mom said she couldn't stand it much longer, the way they surrounded her, all the time and on every side. Gramma down below every minute and hour of the day, and this simp of a husband who couldn't even keep track of where he left his glasses, his wallet and keys. Looking around like he was so helpless. Like a little boy. Like an infant.

Used to be, she said, that he had some backbone. Wasn't a spineless coward when she first knew him. Saw him on a stool at the Eight Ball in Brighton, and looked like a nice guy who knew how to enjoy himself.

Had a close shave and wore a starched white shirt, with the button at the collar open. Smiled at her when she sat down.

And what did she have back then? A job in a factory, putting belts through belt loops on skirts and pants, then boxing them, twenty-four to a box, box after box, and that bastard, Mr. Willeford, the foreman who always needed a shave and had tobacco and onions on his breath. Saying, Very nice, and staring at her chest, at her tatas, and winking, and that breath could make a goat faint, in the name of Jesus and the Twelve Apostles.

So she sat down, and Bill smiled at her after a while, and they each had a gin and tonic with a slice of green lime floating at the top of the crescent ice cubes.

Said he'd been in the Army, in South Carolina and Texas and on Long Island. Here and there—on base hospitals, and they'd ship the soldiers and sailors back from all parts of the world, wrapped head to foot in white bandages. And the burn cases were the worst. Kept picturing the slits in the faces where the eyes stared out from the gauze, and the eyes full of suffering.

Then he said he'd be up at seven the next morning for the eight o'clock Mass—this was Saturday evening and he lived with his mom and dad. And she said she'd be getting up too.

And she had a room on the third floor of a building in Newton Corner, with a hot plate, and down the hall was a bathroom she shared with two other women who worked and didn't have family either.

We sat at the kitchen table on the first floor, and Gramma poured each of us a glass of beer from a brown quart bottle, and she sat down and looked over at me and smiled.

I didn't know, she said, how good I had it. My own little place up there on the third floor, and nothing to do all day except watch television and listen to the radio and eat chocolate doughnuts if I damn well pleased.

Get the welfare to pay the rent and food stamps for groceries and pills to wake up and go to sleep and stay calm and tranquil all through the day. Fill out a form or two and keep your nose clean and never have to work a day in your life. Even had a nice little car and could go out and drive around at three in the morning, for God's sake.

But your mother, Gramma said. She came from nowhere. From the nuns in New York City, down there during the Depression. And Bill was just living with us, with me and your grandfather in Newton Corner, minding his business, and she walked in and saw him sitting at a bar.

A bar, for the sake of Jesus and Mary and Joseph.

Him with the whisky and gin and vodka.

And what kind of people do you think her mother and father were?

People too lazy to work. People who would abandon a child in New York City, and nobody to look after her. Then the nuns took her in.

When I locked the door, the third floor was quiet, and I could sleep sometimes twelve or fourteen or sixteen hours in a day. Could wake up at five in the evening and the sun was growing pale and weak in the west, and I could hear the vibrations from the television downstairs.

I'd go from window to window, room to room, looking out at the gathering darkness. I'd see a church steeple a mile away, and in the sky in the east I'd see the buildings of downtown Boston.

The bottles of pills were lined up on a table in the front room, then in the kitchen, and I'd take two Valiums, two Fiorinals, two codeines, then I sipped a warm can of beer, in the swallowing darkness, and after a half hour or an hour, and with squares of yellow light in the windows of surrounding houses, I'd begin to feel tired again.

Sometimes I'd take an X-acto knife, and I'd sit in the big chair in the front room, and I'd begin to trace lines with the knife on my forearms. Barely touching the skin, I'd make lines on the insides of my wrists, and I'd trace the skin up to the elbow, leaving a thin line of red. Then I'd take my pants off, and I'd make lines on my legs as well.

I could feel the sting, but it was dull, and with only the light from the moon and streetlight out front, the red lines would deepen and grow black, and would then fade to invisible in the dark. Then there was only a stinging trace on my arms and legs.

I'd sip beer, take more pills, then I'd make more cuts on my arms and legs. I'd lie back in the chair, staring at the walls and ceiling.

Then I got dressed, in long-sleeved shirts, in pants and sneakers, and I went down the stairs. I knocked at the door to the second floor, and I heard Dad say, Jack? Is that you, Jack?

I said, Yes, and he said, Is everything okay?

Yes, I said, and he let me in. I followed him through the darkened apartment to the living room.

Your mother's asleep, he said, and then he lay down on the couch, and said, Have a seat.

He said, You doing okay, Jack? and I said, Fine.

We worry about you, he said.

Then a car went past, and the light crossed his face. He was lying down, his head propped on a few pillows, his hands folded on his stomach.

I don't feel so good, he said. My stomach, my bowels, they feel crampy, achy.

Then we were quiet a long time. I could hear him breathe, and I could feel the cuts on my arms and legs stinging. And I could feel the beer and pills too.

There's something lonely about late Sunday nights, he said. You ever feel that?

Something like the last person alive and awake in the world, and everyone else is gone.

He said, I guess you never think like that, but your old man does, all the time now.

We worry about you, Jack, he said. Your mother and your grandmother and me. Keeping strange hours and whatnot.

When I was your age, he said, I joined the Army, and I sometimes think those were the best years of my life. Nineteen years old and thrown in there with the United States of America. With young people my age from every state in the Union. Oklahoma and Nebraska and Oregon.

We knew what was expected of us and we did it. We knew about sacrifice.

Not like today. Everything on a silver platter.

We made mistakes, he said. Sure, we made mistakes.

Your mother used to say that she had never heard of a child like you.

Just staring, hour after hour.

Like you were born old.

Never a peep out of you. Never a smile, a hint of laughter.

Now you're up there—and we hear you walking around at all hours. Creak and creak and creak.

We won't be here forever, he said. This can't go on much longer.

15.

IT'S STILL ALMOST three weeks away, the man in the brown suit says, but they want to be sure that I understand everything that will happen, and that there will be no surprises. Nothing will happen that I do not already know about in advance, and they will do everything in their power to insure that this is a humane and painless procedure.

To begin with, he says, we'll make sure that phone lines stay open in case a pardon or a stay is issued at the last moment, however unlikely that may be.

Everything is being done to insure that every possible means of appeal has remained open, and that in the event of anything last minute, we're prepared to handle that eventuality.

Until midnight, this can be called off, postponed or canceled in an instant. We want you to know that we're prepared to carry out the sentence of the court, but we are every bit as prepared to carry out any alteration in that sentence. In an instant and at a moment's notice. And either eventuality will be carried out in a humane and professional manner.

Because you are already in the holding cell, near the procedure room itself, next door in fact, there will be no need to move you to another cell.

That evening, Father Curran will be able to be with you the entire time leading up to the execution itself. You will be allowed to order a final meal at any time before seven P.M., and the dinner tray will be removed at eight P.M.

At eleven, the guards will ask you to put on a diaper-type garment under your slacks, and at eleven-thirty, you'll be given a shot of an antihistamine to help prevent choking and coughing during the procedure. After that, before we take you to the chamber itself, we'll give you a second shot, of sodium pentothal this time, to help you relax somewhat.

We will also have hooked up an intravenous line in your arm, and that will carry a saline solution into your veins that will help the other drugs move more readily and effectively into your bloodstream.

A group of guards will take you next door into the chamber itself, and Father Curran will give you his final blessing as they secure you to the chair. The chair will look very much like the modern reclining chairs dentists use in their offices. The intravenous line will then be hooked on the injection-delivery module.

The curtains will be opened onto the witness-viewing area, and the order of execution will be read. You will then be able to make a brief final statement. When the second hand on the clock reaches midnight, a button is pushed at two different stations on the module, one of which will activate the machine. Neither of the two people pushing the buttons on the module will ever know which of the two actually activated the machine.

At this point, the procedure is under way. And once more, I want to assure you, there will be no surprises, and we expect that you will feel no physical discomfort whatsoever.

At precise intervals, the machine will deliver three drugs into your body. The first drug will be sodium pentothal, the same drug which you will have been given prior to leaving this cell for the execution chamber. Only now, the machine will deliver fifteen cc of a two-percent solution of sodium pentothal to you, roughly double the earlier dose. The injection itself will take ten seconds, and the machine will then wait for one minute, by which time you will no longer be conscious and you will no longer feel pain.

Following the one-minute wait, the machine delivers fifteen cc of pancuroniom bromide in ten seconds, and then waits for one minute. Pancuronium bromide is a very powerful muscle relaxant that will stop your heart and help arrest your respiratory system.

After another one-minute pause, fifteen cc of potassium chloride, a heart medicine, will be injected, and death will occur within two minutes.

He looks down at his notes, and then looks up at my eyes. His eyes are brown and steady.

We want you to know that this is not a job, a task, that we relish. But because the law of the Commonwealth now exists, and has existed, and the courts have ordered it, we are prepared to carry out the execution, but to do it, as I said before, in as dignified and painless and professional a manner as possible.

Father Curran is wearing a maroon V-neck sweater today, and his hands seem almost blue. He gives me a small box of chocolates, and when I pause with them in my hands, he says, Go ahead.

Mrs. Marcham, the housekeeper and cook at the rectory where Father Curran lives, bought them and asked him to give them to me.

She's a good soul, he says.

I haven't tasted chocolate in years, and am amazed at the pleasure it seems to give my mouth.

How are you doing? he asks, and I shrug.

He nods at the box and says, Thank God for the small pleasures, huh?

I offer the box to him, and he takes one, chews silently.

Finally he says, Are you thinking about it much? The thing itself? The final hour?

I shake my head. Then nod.

I think about it all the time now, he says, and don't ask me why. I think about my own end quite a bit too.

He says that he's seventy-five, and he's already had one heart attack. A mild one, thank the Lord, but a heart attack nevertheless.

That's what took my own father. John Francis Curran, he says. In 1964. He was listening to a Red Sox game on the radio, and he fell out of his chair onto the dining room floor. July seven. A Tuesday it was that year. My mother was in the backyard, and when she came in and found him, she said he looked like he was sleeping, he seemed so much at peace.

Imagine, he says. Thinking a thing like that.

My brother Mark always said the Red Sox killed Dad, he says, and laughs softly.

They would, you know. A team like that. Year after year.

He looks down at his hands and then puts a hand on the handcuff on my wrist.

An old man like me, he says. I've been around a long time. Had a long life, a good life, God knows.

His eyes are blue, and red and yellow at the edges. There are folds of skin under his eyes.

I asked God to call me, when I was a very young man, when I was practically a boy, and he did, I think. I prayed and prayed to be called to his service, and I believe he did.

I don't think I could say that I've ever regretted it. Not really, anyway.

There have been moments, and sometimes there was loneliness. You spend a long long time, in the company sometimes of other priests, in the company of your parishioners. But you go to bed alone, every night of your life, and you wonder about intimacy. Just touching another human being.

He pauses.

Not sex, so much. Not the act of physical sexuality, but the closeness, the touching itself. There are moments when it feels like your skin is craving it, is thirsting for even the merest touch. And it doesn't occur, of course, and so you pray and pray for peace.

He looks at my hands, and folds his own hands in his lap.

I shouldn't go on so, he says. You're the one in Gethsemane, and like His companions, I've fallen asleep on you, have left you by yourself, to pass the night in a kind of prayer.

He watches my face for a minute or more. He smiles.

As a priest, he says, you get called to participate in the major events in people's lives.

Their births and marriages and deaths. You perform the sacraments of the church, you bless and anoint and help them along for a time on their way.

And now I think of you, John Connor, and this peculiar event, and I think how you now know the hour of your end, and that is something almost none of us can ever know, is it? Even a soldier, before battle, has hope that he will survive, doesn't he?

Now I turn on the television and I open the *Globe* and I see it everywhere. I turn on the radio in the car, and they say, It's now twenty-one days till the final day in the life of convicted killer John Connor, and authorities are proceeding with preparations as though this event were not a rarity in the Commonwealth, something that has not occurred here in more than half a century.

I hear that, he says, and I'm seventy-five years old, and my heart is weak just as my father's was. And I wonder, Am I any different from you, except in the knowing? In the night and the time and the means?

Long Time Ago

16.

DURING THE DAY, they were nice to him. They gave him cookies and milk and had him sit at the kitchen table, either downstairs at Gramma's, or in the second-floor kitchen, and they told him that he was a nice boy, a smart boy, a well-behaved boy, and handsome as the day was long.

Grandpa said that when he was a little boy—not much older than you, he said to Jack—his momma made popcorn and heated some milk on the stove, then poured the milk into a cup and sprinkled nutmeg on top. Then Grandpa, as a little boy, with his mom and pop, would gather by candlelight or sputtering gaslight in the long, dark living room of their house over to Watertown, and Momma and Poppa would tell stories about the old country, about Ireland, where they had come from many years earlier, when they were just teenagers.

In Ireland, there were many brothers and sisters, and they grew turnips on the farm that was no bigger than a postage stamp, and the ground was filled with rocks, everywhere and all the time.

Life was hard in Ireland because of the rent on the land, and a man came on horseback to collect the rent, which was baskets of turnips, and there was almost nothing left over to eat or sell. His grandmother, Grandpa said, had gray hair and was bent over and toothless long before her time.

But there was a fire in the hearth, a fire of peat, which was a part of the earth itself, and they told stories there too, just as years later, in Watertown, they told stories.

How at night, in the shadows, in dreams and darkness, when you thought you were sleeping safe and warm in your bed, there were ghosts and fairies and elves and brownies and sprites, moving about in the darkness and quiet.

Dad came in with a brown bottle and sat down, and he lit a cigarette.

By then, Jack had already eaten and taken his bath and changed into pajamas, and it was no longer light outside the windows, out front on Clifton Street, or in the backyard, or anywhere. There were bats flying outside in the warm dark air, squeaking and blind.

In some stories, Grandpa said, bats turned into vampires, and vampires were like people who had risen out of their coffins in graveyards anyplace in the world, and they walked slowly down country lanes and in the back alleys of cities, looking for an open window, and a sleeping maiden or child. The moonlight would be falling through an open window, through the screen on the window, and would spill like powder on the pale necks and faces of maidens and children.

A maiden, Dad said, was a young girl of thirteen or fourteen, and then he sipped at his bottle and puffed on his cigarette, and that made his face glow red for a second.

They were sitting in the den on the first floor, and there was a dim light on in the corner by the shaded window, and Jack sat on the floor, his knees drawn to his chest.

After a while, Gramma came in. She gave him a glass of ginger ale that had two ice cubes floating on the top, and an etching of a sailboat on the side of the glass. She sat down in her rocking chair and took up her knitting.

Vampires, Grandpa said, had to find a sleeping maiden or a sleeping child, and they had to do it during the night, by biting them in the neck, and then that person turned into a vampire too. And they had to be back in their coffin before sunrise. If they were caught outside by the sunlight, they would die.

Mom came in and sat down in a chair by the radiator. She crossed her arms on her chest, and smiled at Jack.

The only way to protect against a vampire, Grandpa said, was to hold up a cross so the vampire could see it. Christ on the cross. Christ nailed on the cross, and suffering and bleeding and dying for all of our sins.

And that includes your sins, young man, Gramma said.

For God's sake, Dad said, and laughed. This sounds like a butcher shop, for the love of God.

Gramma said that vampires were just in stories that people made up to explain certain things. That nobody was really raised from the dead, only in stories.

Except for Christ in the Bible, Dad said. On the third day he arose again. That was Easter, in the springtime, right when all the flowers and trees were bursting with life again, after the death of winter.

They were quiet for a minute or two. A clock ticked in the hall, and cars went by on the street out front. Somewhere outside, a door slammed.

Gramma said, They say that there were people who were like vampires, long ago in Europe. People who snuck around at night, and tried to dig up bodies in graveyards.

She knitted, the needles clicking quietly.

And the Lord knows, people do strange and cruel things to one another, Gramma said.

There was a man not too long ago, named Albert Fish, she said, in New York.

The Moon Maniac, Grandpa said, and Mom said, Wasn't he executed at Sing Sing?

Gramma nodded. Winter, 1936, I think. It scared the bejesus out of me. What he did to children.

He could hear each of them breathe. Slow, deep breaths that filled the corners of the room.

He had watery eyes, Gramma said, and he was far worse than any vampire, let me tell you. He had a beard, and he was sixty-three years old when they caught him, and they only caught him because he wrote an anonymous letter to the family of a little girl he had taken six years earlier.

He used to dance naked in the moonlight, chanting, I am Christ, I am Christ, I am Christ, Gramma said.

He was brought up in an orphanage, she went on, and he later claimed that everything bad in him began there. He said, I saw so many boys whipped, it took root in my head. He said, Misery leads to crime.

They took an X-ray, and found that he had put twenty-nine sewing needles into his own groin. He carried around what he called his instruments of hell—a saw, a butcher knife, a cleaver.

He liked children, Gramma said.

I'll never forget the headlines, Mom said, when they caught him. "The Thrill Vulture." "The Moon Maniac." "The Vampire Man," they called him.

And when he was sentenced to be electrocuted at Sing Sing, Gramma said, he said, It will be the supreme thrill, the only one I haven't tried.

Dad said, C'mere, honey, and patted his knee, and Jack climbed into his lap.

Dad brushed his nose through Jack's hair. This was all a very long time ago, he said. Do you understand that?

Jack nodded.

They're all long gone, all those people, Dad said.

And the fairies and ghosts and vampires, Gramma said, are just stories people tell to scare each other around the fire at night.

Think of angels, Dad said, especially when you're going to sleep. Think of your guardian angel hovering over you.

Gramma said, We're always here anyway, and Grandpa and Mom laughed.

Later, when he was walking up the steps to the third floor, he kept trying to think of an angel with wings, and he tried to make his thoughts be careful.

He pulled the covers over his head and tried to stop his own breathing, but after thirty or forty seconds, he couldn't hold out any longer, and he gasped at the air. Then he folded his hands and prayed quickly. He said five Our Fathers, five Hail Marys, and ten Acts of Contrition.

He could hear footsteps down below. He heard water running, and he heard a cabinet door closing, and it seemed as though a spot in the floor or wall sighed. He blinked his eyes and turned over, facing the two windows. The curtains were bleached with moonlight.

Then it was later, and he knew he had been asleep. There were footsteps moving slowly down the hall toward his room—and as they got closer, they moved even more slowly. He blinked, and there was a figure in white standing in the doorway.

Jackie, his mother whispered. Jackie, she hissed.

He closed his eyes and tried not to move, and he heard her walk slowly across the room to his bed.

You sleeping? she asked. You out like a light?

Her voice was husky and slow. It seemed as though someone had oiled her tongue and throat. Her tongue slipped on words.

Your gramma scare you? she asked. She put the fear of God in you?

She was quiet, and he heard ice cubes tap glass, he heard her swallow.

It's nothing, she said. Those people. The weird ones. They're not gonna touch you.

You have a mom and dad, a gramma and grandpa. And they only hurt the ones who have nobody to protect them.

Albert Fish won't get you, she said. Albert Fish killed and ate his last little child a long time ago. And he won't be doing that anymore. Not where he is. In the fires for eternity.

Howling like a hungry wolf, she said.

Because after a while, God has no mercy anymore. God runs out of patience.

She chuckled. Believe me, she said. I know.

She sat on the bed, and leaned her back against the wall.

When cars passed, their headlights made angles of light cross the ceiling. They were moving fast, and were going a long way away. They were tired, and wanted to be home.

Mom said, The nuns didn't think much of little orphan girls, in New York City, back there in the 1920s and '30s.

You don't understand anything, she said, and she began to cry quietly. Sniffling and making small choked sounds.

Nobody knows what that was like, she said, and he heard her wipe away tears with her hands.

She sipped, and wiped tears, and cried some more. She breathed quickly, and he listened to her, and after a while her breathing slowed a little.

Her father was almost never there, in New York City, back in those years. It was just her and her mother, in rooms, and in hallways that were always dark and smelled of pee and sweat and dirty dishes.

Always holes in the curtains and bedspreads, and springs coming through the chair and mattress.

Water stains, spiders, cockroaches everywhere.

Her mother was old and gray and tired all the time. She coughed, and sometimes when she coughed there was blood on her hands and on the piece of newspaper she used as a handkerchief.

And after I'm gone, her mother said to her, you'll be sorry you didn't appreciate me when I was here.

Once in a great while a man with white hair came to visit them. He smelled like boiled potatoes and peppermint and medicine, and he talked in a whispery voice.

I'm your pop, he said to her in a low, scraping voice, then he laughed softly.

He never lived with us, Mom said, and he always seemed to be out of a job. Then when we were living in a room over on the west side, somewhere near the river, I remember hearing that he died, and they buried him in Potter's Field, where they put all the homeless and poor.

Just this big field of unmarked graves, near the edge of the harbor. Seagulls coming down, and boats passing out on the water, and foghorns moaning late at night.

Just loneliness, Mom said. Just loneliness and emptiness and anonymity.

And it wasn't long after that, she said, that her mother brought her to the nuns, and they were not much fun either, believe you me. Being an orphan in an orphanage, just like Albert Fish had been.

She put her hand on his hair, then on his shoulder.

You're a lucky boy, she said. A lucky lucky boy.

Then there was only quiet, and car lights a million miles away. Going by, and the wood in the walls and floors sighing some more.

Something whispering and saying his name almost too softly to hear. And an old man with a kind face and soft wet eyes. Wearing a long dark overcoat, and baggy pants and black rubber boots. Carrying a dark cloth bag and smiling.

Saying, My child, my sweet young child.

Don't be afraid, he said, in such a low voice that Jack seemed almost to drift into the warm sound.

Come with me, the man said, and they were riding in a train through New York City. This was when his mom, Jack's mom, was just a little girl herself, going to an orphanage.

But this was different too, Jack knew. This was the same time as then, because all the cars were black, and everything was faintly dark as in an old photograph.

In the city, men and women, children with large eyes, were sleeping in parks, on benches and under trees and bushes. They were standing in the rubble of vacant lots, among broken bricks and dusty boards, around a small fire in a trash barrel.

Then Jack was walking on a country road at night, first by himself, then with an old man who carried a black cloth bag. The old man's voice was low and steady as a prayer, and Jack felt as though he was in church almost.

The stars at night, the man said, are very beautiful. In the black sky.

They're jewels, he said. They're like the eyes of angels, all sparkle and shine.

They're dark flowers, like the eyes of children.

And the moon draws us up to her cold surface, he whispered. She draws us upward.

They went by tall whispering trees, and dark fields, and over hills and through valleys.

He wore a long overcoat, and the fields were no longer cold, and they smelled like earth and flowers.

Everything is with God and through God, the man whispered.

Everything he made, in his wisdom and his sadness.

Suffer the little children to come unto me, the man said, and he smiled his slow gentle smile, and then there was a path that went off from the road they were walking on, and they turned into it and went through woods.

Far ahead, between the trees, Jack could see a small farmhouse, its windows boarded up, in a small clearing.

God made children, the man said, the fruit of his kingdom, the flower of his loins.

He said the sky and the air, the night, the moon, the stars, were as deeply beautiful, as full of wonder and magic and awe, as anything in creation.

Look, the old man said, and pointed to the stars in the black sky.

The eyes of children, just shining up for all the world to see. In his kingdom of heaven.

His voice was low, and it was music, and Jack was more sleepy and peaceful than he had ever been in his life. As though he was high above, and as distant as heaven.

17.

GROWING UP IN Ithaca, New York, with parents on the faculty at Cornell—one in English, one in physics—I didn't come across many people like John Connor. Or maybe I should say that if I did come across such people, I didn't exactly notice or remember them. And that is my fault, of course. That is one of the limitations of my background.

Because there were kids like that. Kids with pale skin and ill-fitting, infrequently washed clothes who came to school on buses, from out in the rural areas of Tompkins County. They were often kids who lived in trailers, or in little more than shacks, and in a few cases I heard of, lived in abandoned school buses.

But to compare Connor to those kids, to the rural poor, is to miss the point also, and that is what I have been trying these last months not to do. That is my job here at the *Boston Globe*. To get as many of the facts as I can, and to stitch them together into a more or less coherent picture. And from this picture, our readers will be able to make some sense out of something it's not possible to understand—at least not in the terms we normally use to understand events.

So I tell myself, Connor was like those kids who came to school in Ithaca in buses, and even though I barely noticed or talked to those kids, I think I can imagine their lives. Going home to a trailer, to a mother on welfare. A mother who is overweight, who smokes and drinks, who never married the father of her children. The father is now long gone, and during the day, when the children are at school, the mother stays inside in the trailer and watches television, smokes and drinks, eats potato chips and cheese sandwiches and chocolate chip cookies out of a package.

Connor is like those kids in the sense that from everything I've been able to learn, he was a marginal kid. Someone with virtually no friends, who came and went on the edges of school life. A kid who was pale, and whose clothes were never quite right. Whose shirts were too big or too small, were maybe torn or patched or stained. The kid in gym class who didn't have white socks and sneakers, and so he wore black socks and brown shoes, which stood out because his bare legs were so white, and every other kid had white socks and sneakers. And because of the shoes, he was always sliding on the floor of the gym or outside on the grass. And he always fell down, trying to play basketball or rounding the bases during a game of softball or kickball. And God knows, the other kids must have laughed.

I don't know, of course. I just have no idea what it is or was like for him. To do what he did, and now to face what he faces.

I've been at the *Globe* almost three years, and I came here from the *Ithaca Journal*, and I went to the *Journal* from the *Cornell Daily Sun*, so it's not as though I've been out here in the world for a huge long time, having this great breadth of experience.

Ithaca is in upstate New York, about midway between Syracuse and Binghamton, in what they call the central southern tier. It's set among hills, some of which are pretty high, in the Finger Lakes region, which is a series of long, thin lakes. The Indians used to say that the lakes were made a long time ago, when God pressed his fingers onto the face of the earth.

There are three major hills surrounding the city. And on two of the hills are educational institutions—Ithaca College on South Hill and Cornell University on East Hill.

There are all kinds of restaurants—Indian, Vietnamese, Thai—good local theaters for movies and plays, good bookstores, and spectacular natural surroundings. There are gorges and waterfalls all over the place, and working farms five minutes out of town. But if you come in-town and walk on the Commons, this pedestrian mall downtown, you can easily hear conversations in half a dozen languages in the space of two blocks.

There are at least two people on the faculty at Cornell who have won Nobel Prizes, the best English department in the country, or so my mother will claim, and maybe the most beautiful university campus anywhere, or so Cornell's public affairs department will claim.

Even though my mom is an English professor and my dad teaches physics, they were always telling me that most of the world was not like Ithaca and Cornell, and they encouraged me to explore those other parts of the world. So I majored in English, and actually took an Emily Dickinson seminar with Mom. But I also wrote for the *Daily Sun*, and that was great.

The *Sun* is Cornell's daily newspaper, but it has its offices downtown, away from the university, and that's pretty important. When you work on the *Sun*, you tend to stay up until three every morning, and everything's always on deadline. So you kind of get the flavor of real newspaper life. Even if what you're writing about is contract negotiations between the university and an employees union, or allegations that some professor sexually harassed some students.

After I graduated, I wanted to stay in Ithaca while my boyfriend Richard finished law school, so I worked at the *Ithaca Journal*, doing city government, arts, and finally cops, which was the most interesting and fun for me. Being on cops meant that you compiled the crime beat stories—basically a listing of arrests, usually of DWIs and burglary and drug possession.

There were several murders, and the usual car wrecks and cases of arson and lots of welfare fraud. In a strange way, I got kind of addicted to cops. To how different it was from anything I'd ever known and the life I'd grown up in. And I also came to think that cops did an amazing and difficult job, and that they almost never got credit for their work.

I'd grown up with the standard prejudice against cops, thinking they were too often bullies and power freaks. But in Ithaca, and then here in Boston, the more time I spent with them, the more I began to see that they do incredibly difficult and dangerous work, and that they almost always do it with grace and restraint and skill. And they rarely get thanked. They see ugliness all the time. They come into the house where kids have been almost starved to death. They talk to a woman who's been beaten by her boyfriend. They deal with drunks and crazies, with people who've been robbed or assaulted or raped, and they do it almost every shift they work.

When I hear that cops have these really high rates of divorce, ulcers, alcoholism, and suicide, I don't feel in the least bit surprised. And when I hear of cases of cops beating suspects or falsifying evidence or taking bribes, I'm always kind of struck by how relatively rare that is.

Anyway, when Richard finally finished law school, he and I both came here to Boston. And because of a former classmate of my father's at Harvard, I had these interviews at the *Globe*, and I was hired about a month after moving here.

I've done mostly general reporting, but about two months ago I began to do quite a bit of legwork for Martin Wallace, one of the *Globe*'s really big writers, working on the Connor case. And I guess it's a little like being an intern in an emergency room, and having the results of a head-on crash between a pickup truck and a car full of high school kids come in. It's the most tragic, awful moment in the lives of these kids and their families, but for the intern, maybe the single greatest opportunity in her entire education. She's going to see more problems and more medicine in the next twenty-four hours than she's seen in the previous six months. She'll see seventeen-year-old kids with massive head injuries, with broken bones and contusions and lacerations, and everything will happen real fast too. One or two of the kids will be up and out of the hospital within a few weeks, another will be dead within a few days. None of it's fair, of course. It's never, ever fair.

So that's what I've been often thinking about the Connor case. That in late August 1988, during one of the hottest summers on record in the northeast United States, and for much of the rest of the country, this thirty-four-year-old man, John Emmanuel Connor, a former mental patient who seems to have rarely worked and who seems to have almost never left his parents' home, killed his mother, father, and paternal grandmother, apparently while they were asleep in their beds at home.

Connor had no previous criminal record, and the entire Connor family seems to have had little contact with the rest of the world. I've knocked on doors, made dozens of phone calls, and talked to scores of people who have known, even fleetingly, this family, and I can get almost nothing.

They were quiet, people say. Polite. Paid their bills on time. Never caused anyone any problems.

The father had a spotty work record, and seems to have gone away for weeks or months at a time, but nobody seems to know where he went or what he did.

And on several occasions, John, the son, seems to have left the house in Newton for short periods of time, but he seems to have always returned. And there, too, I can't figure out where he went or why or what he did. Just that he was gone for a few weeks, and then he came back.

We have a high school yearbook photo, and I talked to one teacher of his from high school who said he was a bright enough kid, but that he was very isolated, or so it seemed to her. *Friendless* is the word she used.

I spoke to a neighbor, someone who lived just down the street from the Connor home in Newton, and he kept saying how Newton was a great place to raise kids, and something like this was an aberration and shouldn't be on the front pages of every newspaper in the country. Think how this will stigmatize families who have experienced mental illness, this man said, and I thought he was right, of course, that this was a strange, aberrant story, and was certainly atypical. But that's why it's news. And maybe reporting the story would help families seek help for mentally ill children or parents or siblings.

I don't know. Probably that's a lot of self-serving, sanctimonious drivel. Sometimes I think reporters are as bad as politicians. We talk about what we do in the most high-minded, elevated way, as though we walk a brave and lonely road, and our sole purpose is to serve the public interest. And that we do it selflessly, at great personal sacrifice. That we don't make the money doctors and lawyers do—unless we're on television, and that's more show business than journalism—and that nobody gives us the proper credit.

But just about every newspaper I've ever heard of has an unspoken motto: If it bleeds, it leads. The crime, the crash, the fire, the disaster will almost always make it to the top of the front page. It's what people want to read.

Martin Wallace, who's been doing this a lot longer than I have, doesn't seem to be bothered by any of this. Get the goods, he says. Gather string.

By which he means, talk to lots of people, keep as many lines of communication open as possible, and we'll get enough information and impressions to put some kind of picture, however patchy or out of focus, before the public.

With Connor, it's very difficult and frustrating. This will be the first use of capital punishment in Massachusetts since around the time of the Depression and World War II. That's a very long time, and it also gives this case a kind of *High Noon*, showdown-at-the-stroke-of-midnight or noon feel. Even though Connor has exhausted his appeals and is supposedly reconciled to his fate. The law was passed in early 1988, but nobody ever thought it would actually be carried out, not in this state.

You still have the room at Cedar Junction, the chair or table he'll be strapped down in, and these witnesses watching the whole thing through a window, as though this is TV. And the strangest thing is, I'll be there.

Martin asked me, and he was decent enough to say, Don't give me an answer until tomorrow. He'll be there, and some other reporters, and a priest who's been meeting with Connor.

I talked to Richard, half of one night, it seemed, and then I talked to my mother. I kept thinking, If I say no, it'll be because I'm a woman, and people will say, She may be a reporter, but she's still a woman, she doesn't have a pair of balls. So even though the idea of the execution kind of makes me sick to my stomach, as though I'm going to throw up or pass out or something, another part of me feels as though this will be the biggest and most dramatic moment of my career.

As though I can't not do this. As though there's no way I could ever say no and then look myself in the eye ever again.

So I told Martin, Sure, I want to be there, and he smiled and patted me on the shoulder and said, Of course you do.

I thought of that later, of what he said, and I wanted to ask him what he meant. As though he knew all along that I'd want to be there. As though he thought of me as this cold-blooded, ambitious little shit of a reporter who would never miss the opportunity to advance my career. And so what if some sorry bastard was being killed by the state—as long as I could make my bones, so to speak. As long as I could move up and over and along.

But I don't know. Maybe that was only my own voice, telling me to be a good little girl, a demure girl, without steel or ambition. Either way I'm screwed, right?

And Martin's more complicated anyway. He wouldn't have asked me to work the Connor case, and to get Johnson, the managing editor, to go along with it, if he really didn't think much of my work.

So I've been busting my ass and getting almost nowhere, and feeling frustrated and excited as hell, all at the same time.

People in the halls and in the newsroom see me, and they want to stop to talk. I see people at the Corrections Department or the Attorney General's office, people from TV, from the networks, from New York, D.C., and L.A., and they know who I am, and that I work for the *Globe* and for Martin Wallace, and they say, How you doing? What's up? You hear this or that?

And I know Martin made his bones with busing, back in the seventies, when he was even younger than me. And now it's my turn.

So I stare at this high school picture of John Connor, and I get on the phone, and I look at the screen on my computer and at my pages and pages of notes.

Has little to say, I write. Very quiet. Cooperative.

At Cedar Junction, the spokesperson, a woman named Lampkin, says that Mr. Connor is composed and at peace with himself. She tells us that he ate tuna fish and broccoli, or hot dogs and carrots. That he has a Bible in his cell, and very few personal possessions. We say that it's twenty-five days away, or twenty-one, or less than three weeks.

At one point I got a call from a woman in Ohio who knew Connor from a one-nighter in her town. She met him in a bar several years earlier, I gather, was going through some kind of bad patch of her own at the time, and brought him home.

She said it was only the one night, but that he had been very sweet. That was the word she used. She said when she saw a story and picture of Connor in her local paper, about the sentence finally being carried out, she knew it was him, and that's how she ended up calling here at the *Globe*. We get tons of nuts calling every week, but Madden, the kid who answers the phones up here, put this one through because he said she sounded for real, somehow.

I think she was, only she couldn't shed a whole lot of light on the subject. Just that he was quiet and sweet, and that he drove out of her life the next morning.

And I keep thinking I'll figure it out. Understand what made him do what he did.

Because he drank or used too many prescription drugs. Because he was so lonely and isolated and desperate. Because there were voices in his head.

What about the grandmother, who was over ninety years old, lying there in her bed? Was she even awake? Did she have any idea at all?

Or the father or mother? Did they look up in the dark and see him walking into the room? Was he standing at the end of the bed? Sobbing? Smiling?

Then I think that in late August 1988, I had just returned to Ithaca after traveling in Europe with my friend Tamar. We went to something like nine countries, and everywhere we went there were these amazing things for us to see and do and taste and remember. This Greek island where the sky and the water were so blue they almost hurt our eyes. And we swam nude, and then lay on these huge rocks in the sun.

By late August, we were back in Ithaca, about to start our senior year at Cornell. Now Tamar is in San Francisco, finishing the second year of her residency. She'll probably go into pediatrics.

On a Saturday night, late that August, I might have been at a party, dancing and laughing. There, with all my friends, with my last, best year of college still in front of me.

18.

I MOVED THROUGH the darkness of their apartment like air, and they slept deeply, slept like babies after a long feeding. On the first floor, Gramma lay in bed, her fists curled to her chest. The bureaus in her bedroom were tall and made of dark wood, and the light fell from the moon and stars in the sky, and far away, on the other side of life, it seemed, a church clock tolled three times.

On the second floor they slept in the same bed, and even though the floor in the hall creaked under my weight, they didn't move or stir. He slept on his back, his arms down at his sides, and she slept on her left side, curled away from him.

They didn't know I had keys to their apartments, but I had had the keys so long, I almost couldn't remember when I had got them. Back during high school, perhaps, when I had taken a spare key from a hook behind the pantry door, or from under a corner of the mat in the hall, and brought them to a hardware store to have copies made.

And when Gramma got mad and said, You don't watch out, little man, you'll go back there, and this time they won't let you out so easy—when she said that to me, her voice as hard and edged as flint, I never said anything or even smiled.

The summer of 1988 was hotter and drier than anything I'd ever known. Every day, almost, the temperatures rose into the eighties, then kept rising through the morning, until by noon it was ninety already, and still moving up. For three or four days the afternoon temperatures would reach ninety-six, ninety-four, ninety-seven, then ninety-four again, and on the radio the voices said there would be a shower late at night, and for a day or two things would cool down to the upper eighties, but with the humidity remaining high.

I slept much of the day, with a fan going slowly back and forth in the bedroom on the third floor. But even with the fan, it was as though I had a constant fever, and I'd wake up to pee, and I'd soak my hair and neck with cold water from the faucet. I'd take a few pills, two Valiums, say, a Fiorinal or two, then I'd lie in bed again and try not to move, even a hand or finger, and I'd make myself breathe slowly and I'd think of ice and snow and wind blowing down from the north, and after a while I'd fall asleep again, and wake up a long time later, when the room was dark, and windows everywhere were open.

Dad said he couldn't always remember much. He tried and tried, and he could remember something about being a very young boy, maybe three or four years old and being lost, at night, somewhere out in the country. He had been with his mother or father, or with his father's brother, Uncle Bernie, and then suddenly it was nighttime and very dark, and he was on a road way far away from anything that seemed familiar. There was a road, and fields and trees, and the sky—he could still picture the sky—it was so full of stars, millions and millions of stars that seemed to glow and dance and twinkle, that he thought this must be some different form of sky.

Uncle Bernie, Dad said, drank too much and often didn't shave. He smoked Camel cigarettes, and he could blow smoke rings out of the circle of his mouth, three white rings that floated through the air like magic, then disappeared.

One time his uncle had to be in a special hospital on account of not feeling too good. On account of the blues and sadness and feeling like crying all the time, and he remembered that he went with his father on buses, first through parts of Boston, then out into the country, until they came to the hospital. His father said to him, Stay close to me, when they finally arrived at the hospital. There were buildings spread over some hills, and people walked around in pajamas and some of them had shaved heads, and one woman they passed kept making kissing sounds at him.

Dad said that later, after the first time he drank a lot of liquor, say when he was eighteen or nineteen, and woke up and couldn't remember anything from the night before, he had the feeling that he would someday go to the same kind of special hospital as Uncle Bernie had gone to.

And it kept happening, he said. Even after he was married and living here on Clifton Street—with his mom and dad downstairs, with me, and he'd be working along just fine, driving to work, driving home, then one afternoon he'd stop off for a drink, and he'd order a soda, and the last thing he'd remember was standing there, and everyone around him was drinking beer and gin and whisky, then suddenly he'd wake up in Missouri or Maryland, and a month would have gone by, and he couldn't remember any of it.

What do you do? the woman named Monica asked.

Why did you come here? And who are you? How long will you stay?

She had short dark hair, and she said she did this from time to time, when she was really bored and getting in a rut. She'd go to a bar and sit down, and start to drink. And the first man to approach her who seemed half interesting—who didn't have tattoos, who had all his teeth, who didn't seem too drunk or crazy—she'd talk with. And if after an hour or so, and after a second drink, he still didn't seem too objectionable, she'd invite him back to her place.

She'd been doing this almost five years, maybe two or three times a year. Always when Steve, her boyfriend, was off hunting or fishing with his buddies.

Outside the window, on the back lawn, a dogwood was in bloom, and I thought its blossoms—the white petals open to the night air— were almost painfully vulnerable.

She said, What are you thinking? And she leaned over in the bed and kissed the side of my face.

She said, You're a quiet one. A strange one. You're different than the rest of them.

By dark that summer, in 1988, the temperatures dropped into the mid-eighties, and I went out and through backyards. There were always open windows, with just a screen to let in the cooler air.

I went over fences, and through bushes. Inside houses, the lights were mostly off, just the occasional television set flickering.

Even the cars on the streets moved slowly. I walked for a half hour, for an hour, through neighborhoods where the houses seemed empty.

I went into more backyards, and crept through bushes, and peeked into a living room window where the light was on. An old lady was sitting in front of a television, her chin resting on her chest, her mouth open.

The screen door was open at the back porch. I went in, and everything everywhere was quiet. The kitchen door was locked, but I checked under the doormat, and around the ledge over a window.

Then I felt on the ledge over the door frame, and found a key. It fit into the door, and I opened it quietly, and just stood for two or three minutes.

The only light in the house seemed to be coming from the living room, and after listening, I crouched down, and moved quietly through the kitchen and dining room, into the front hall. The television was louder from there, so I paused again, got down on my hands and knees, and peeked into the living room.

She was still in her chair, and her mouth was still open, but I could see from here that her eyes were closed. I watched her for a long time. Her chest rising slowly, then falling.

Her hair was white, and she was wearing a baggy summer dress with a pattern of flowers on it.

Finally I turned and went back through the dining room, kitchen and porch, and out to the backyard. The air felt so much cooler out there that the hair on my back and arms seemed to stand on end.

Upstairs and inside, life was mostly quiet, almost all the time. I went out to drugstores, to doctors' offices, to the grocery store for cans of soup, for coffee and milk, and every three or four months I went to the welfare office to fill out a form, to meet with a woman who smiled at me and nodded her head. Every few weeks I went to the bank to make a deposit or cash a check, and I stopped to put gas in the car as well.

When I went out during the day, I was careful to wear tan chinos, blue or yellow Oxford shirts, dark socks, penny loafers. I wore my glasses and made sure I was shaved and that my hair was combed, my teeth brushed. I always took a shower before I went out. I used deodorant, aftershave lotion, I gargled for my breath. I was always pleasant to store clerks, bank tellers, to the staff of the welfare office. I smiled, said, How are you today? Looks like spring is finally coming.

Gramma said her father was like a saint almost, and that everyone who knew him said that as well. Talked about his even temper, his good nature, his kindness and generosity.

I never heard him raise his voice in his life, she said. Not once. Even later, after he was sick and in pain all the time. From the cancer eating away at the tissue of his body. At his lungs and bones, and finally at his brain.

Lying in bed, in that dark room, with just a sliver of washed light at the edge of the curtains. Her mother coming in and out with trays of food and medicine, and the Olson girl they hired to help Mother out. Moving fast and making no noise. But at the end, as he got thinner and thinner, and his hands and arms seemed to curl into themselves like a baby's, and his breath grew more labored and shallow at the same time, she knew he didn't have much time left. And even though she was only eight years old, which wasn't much more than a little kid, she said she could see a darkness and heaviness gathering over her mother like storm clouds, just as everything near her father seemed to take on light and air.

Gramma said the pain seemed to get worse for him, and he whimpered and winced, and her mother or Christine Olson would fill a syringe, and slide the needle into the muscle on his hip, and ten or twenty minutes later they could feel him relax, and whisper to people none of them had ever known or heard of. To Ned, to Sissy, to Liam and Austin.

People, Gramma said, from his earlier life, across the water, on the other side.

This time, she said, she knew he was crossing another great ocean, only now it was an ocean of life and death and time.

Then she woke very late one night, at maybe three or four, and she heard sobs and screams, and she got up and went to the hall, and her mother was sitting on the side of the bed, and she stood and watched, and she swore, she said, it was as though she could see her father's corpse, his spirit, dressed in a long white nightgown, hovering three or four feet above the bed, floating.

And her mother sobbed and hugged the figure in the bed.

So she turned and went back into her own room, and climbed under the bed. Because, she said, she knew there were angels in the house, floating from room to room with her father's pale corpse.

She fell asleep under the bed, and when she woke up, there were strange people in the house, and her father's body was gone. Her mother was lying in the same bed now, right where her father had been, and her eyes were red and stony. And when I went in to hug her, Gramma said, to say how sorry I was, she looked at me as if I wasn't there. Or as if she had gone already.

Gramma looked up from her knitting, and her eyes were wet.

So many of them, in the books, moved around at night, in every part of the country. Went to cemeteries very late, with a pick and shovel, a crowbar, with a knife for cutting.

In Wisconsin, in a country graveyard, a long way from the lights of any town or city, he dug until he hit the wood of the coffin, then he dug away all the earth, and made enough room so he could reach the side and pry open the lid.

Then in the moonlight, he began his work with the corpse, and his mother's grave was so close, so near. Only two or three grave sites away.

In Massachusetts he smiled and knocked on doors, and when they asked through the door who he was and what he wanted, he said he was taking a survey. If I could trouble you for a few minutes of your time, he said.

In Florida he wore a dark watch cap and drove a van, and parked near the school in mid-afternoon. Then the kids came streaming out, in twos and threes, wearing bright clothes, carrying backpacks and plastic or cloth bags for lunches.

In California he was an enormous man, six foot nine, and he weighed three hundred pounds. He had dark hair, wore glasses, and his IQ was 148. His mother was always after him about one thing or another. His size, his smell, his brain, which was not much good for anything except causing trouble. He was like some outsized monster in a fairy story. Some beast that came from underground.

In California, in the book, his mother said he was just like his father, full of dark urges, of unnatural appetites, of weird thoughts and impulses. And you'll end up like him, she said. Alone in a room, with nobody to care for you.

Doofus, she called him. Lurch. Igor.

Frankenstein's monster, she said.

Just look at you. Size-seventeen feet. A head as big as a watermelon. Full of sick thoughts.

So she made him sleep in the basement, in a locked cubicle next to the furnace. When it rumbled and groaned like some beast or something, it began to seem like a part of the inside of him.

Freak that he was, she said.

Wanted to get up during the night and do things to her and his sister.

Just look at you, she said.

And later, in the book, when he had his chance, he would do something to her voice, to her throat, to her vocal chords. Always talking like that to him.

He's always been like that, Mom said. Tired and sad and pretty far away, even when you're sitting right next to him.

When he wasn't drinking, when he wasn't off driving somewhere, to some crazy place or other, he was there, in the house, sitting downstairs with his mother, or in the living room up here.

A million miles away, she said. In his own little world, she said, and there was only room for him and his mother.

You want something to eat, she said. You could fix a can of soup, maybe open some tuna fish, you want it.

After all these years, she said, maybe thirty-five years now, she still didn't know him very well, and that was pretty sad.

You had it good, she said. If I do say so.

Enough to eat, a roof over your head. A few toys, people who looked after you. People who cared whether you were dead or alive.

She didn't have that, she said, and who gave a good goddamn. Not Bill, she said.

He just buried his head in a book. Stared out the window. Said a prayer. Flipped the channels on the television. Went down to his mother's.

She said, You think I had it easy, don't you?

You think that was some kind of picnic for your dear old mom.

New York City was so big that you couldn't even begin to imagine. Glass and steel and brick as far as the eye could see. The wind coming in off the rivers, and the boats and the foghorns.

You think you know what tough-luck kid means, well whoop dee doo. Whoop dee doo.

For you, she said.

Well, goddamn it to hell.

That's what I say, she said.

Goddamn every bit of it to hell. For all eternity.

And don't even think of asking me. Don't even think.

You want to hear about hard times, about tough luck, mister, well then you ask me.

So don't start with me.

Don't think, Mom said.

19.

LITTLE BOYS WERE supposed to keep their mouths shut if they knew what was good for them. They weren't supposed to snoop around and sneak up on people behind their backs. Good little boys, boys who didn't have freckles and blue eyes and dark brown hair.

That's what Gramma said to him, in the back hall on the first floor.

Touching themselves in private places, she said, and what would God and the nuns and priests say if they knew?

You're just like your mother, Gramma said. Lazy and stupid, and pretty ugly too. Ugly freckles all over your face just like dirt. Need to wash the dirt off, and that awful smell. The smell of poverty and squalor.

He blinked and stared at his feet.

She said, Look at me. He kept staring at his feet.

She took his earlobe in her hand and pinched it and lifted his face.

You think I don't know what she says behind my back, don't you? Gramma said. You think I must be stupid or blind like some cripple.

She was quiet, and watching his face. She let go of his ear.

You can't keep a secret either, Gramma said. Can you? Something between two people. Something you're not supposed to tell anyone else.

I'll come for you late, and nobody will even know what happened, she said. Nobody would ever believe it anyway, but there'd be nothing left of you. Just a streak of blood on the sheet. A clump of hair on the pillowcase.

Then she stepped away from him, and he watched her turn and go through the doorway to her kitchen, and slam the door behind her.

Much later, while the wind was blowing outside like it would blow down the house, he heard footsteps and voices chanting things in Latin, the same as in church. They were low voices that seemed to echo in a great space, a space the size of a church.

He was pretty sure he was dreaming, because he looked around and it was dark and he was outside somewhere, in a clearing in the woods. He had been praying, and the sky grew darker and darker. There were streaks of lightning in the distance. Fast and jagged lines of bright light that looked angry.

It began to rain, and the chanting grew louder, and people in red and black and purple robes were filing into the clearing. Each one held a candle in front of him, and then there was a white table, and they circled the table, and he knew he should get out of there. Just as he thought that, a man in a hooded robe looked at him, and as the man turned his face to him, he saw his long nose and glittering eyes, and the candlelight flickered on the surfaces of the man's face, making deep shadows under his eyes and at the side of his nose and mouth.

Jackie, the man said, and his voice was as low as sadness, and he tried to stand up, to turn away.

Jackie, the man said again, and his voice was just as low this time, but there was something cold and edged to the voice too. Something he tried to turn away from.

Then he was in the cellar of their house on Clifton Street, and he was hiding behind boxes. Everything was dark except for a circle of light which shined over a hole. There were clumps of dirt, and he looked carefully around the boxes and over the edge of the hole, and he saw his father, about ten feet down, digging the hole deeper and deeper.

He watched the shovel bite in the dirt, then lift and throw the dirt onto one of the piles at the top of the hole.

His father looked up and squinted, and Jackie was sure for a moment that his father had seen him. Then he heard footsteps on the stairs and he got back behind the boxes.

Gramma came across the cellar, into the circle of light.

You ready? she asked.

His father looked up. Not quite, he said.

She said, He's not going to sleep all night.

On the third floor, in the bedroom, with the wind still blowing outside, he woke up, and he was pretty sure that nothing had happened.

He was breathing quick, shallow breaths, and he listened to the branches of the trees move in the wind. There were no footsteps anywhere, no voices or movement, but he kept listening. His head and chest were burning, and he felt sweat on his forehead and neck.

Get up, get up, someone whispered, and he thought he might be saying that himself.

He thought of the hole in the cellar, and the circle of yellow light hanging over the hole and how it glinted on Gramma's glasses.

He got out of bed, and nearly fainted. There were pins of light, and pinpricks on his arms and legs and back. Everything tingled, and he knew it was a fever.

Then he heard a shovel hitting dirt, and he went to the doorway of his room, and there was nothing in the third-floor hallway. Just a window at the end of the hall.

Hurry, something whispered. Hurry, they're coming.

He got in the closet in the bedroom, behind some old coats that were hanging up, and some blankets that were folded and stacked in the back of the closet.

They'll come, the voice whispered. They're coming now.

But he listened carefully, and all he could hear was the wind.

His whole body began to feel like it was on fire. As though someone was feeding logs into a blazing fire inside of him.

The air in the closet was close and smelled of wool and mothballs, and he closed his eyes and thought he could see the man in the robe, in the candlelight.

Little boy, the man was saying, only now they were in an enormous house, the size of a castle. They were walking down long corridors in the dark. Only the flickering candle lit up the heads of the deer and bears and wild pigs that had been mounted high on the walls.

Finally they came to a series of glass doors that looked out onto a balcony. The balcony was lit by torches, and men and women in evening gowns and tuxedos were standing and talking.

Up above, there were millions of stars in the sky and a crescent moon.

Way off, in a far corner of the balcony, he saw his grandmother, standing and staring at him. She was wearing a lumpy housedress and a cardigan sweater, and she held a rolling pin in her hand. She kept staring at him, but none of the men or women noticed her.

A woman with dark hair piled on her head saw him and smiled. She beckoned to him.

Go ahead, the man in the robe said. She won't hurt you. She's your mother.

But the woman with dark hair looked nothing like his mother. She had pale white skin that glowed, and her dark hair was held in place with silver combs.

John, she said to him. Beautiful boy.

Gramma was glaring at him. There was steam on her glasses and beads of sweat on her forehead and upper lip. He could see a smudge of flour on her sweater.

Gramma didn't say anything, but she didn't look away either. Then behind her, Dad appeared, and he was resting a shovel on his shoulder.

The dark-haired woman wore a long black dress, and a white jacket with a silver cat pin on the lapel.

Don't worry, she said. I've been waiting for you.

She began to walk toward him, almost gliding across the balcony. Gramma and Dad stood and watched him.

He tried the glass door, but it was locked.

He felt a hand on his arm.

Grandpa said, What in the name of God are you doing in here?

Grandpa took him by the arm and pulled him out from behind the blankets and coats. The light in the hall was on, and Gramma was standing in the doorway. Her shadow on the floor of the bedroom was ten feet tall, and she seemed to speak very slowly at first, her voice even lower than a man's voice.

Bill's gone away, she said. Your father has escaped.

Jack thought of the hole, and the shovel and the light over the hole.

Grandpa carried him to the bed and set him down. He felt at Jack's forehead, which was burning.

He's very hot, Grandpa said. He's on fire already.

I'm not surprised, Gramma said. She never feeds him or dresses him properly. No wonder, for the love of God.

Then Gramma turned and went down the long hall. Grandpa pulled the covers up to Jack's neck.

Grandpa said, What were you doing in there?

Grandpa said, It's one in the morning, for the sake of Christ.

He heard Gramma coming back up the steps and down the long hall. She came in and sat on the side of the bed, and she wiped his forehead with a cool, damp facecloth.

Your father's gone, Gramma said. Off in his car. Drunk as midnight.

And your mother, Gramma said, is in no condition to see you.

She's on dope, Gramma said, or she's in a hospital for crazy people and they have bars on all the windows so she can't climb out.

Jack shook his head.

Grandpa said, It's true. All of it. They're both gone, and it's too late now.

Your mother was arrested for lying and stealing, Gramma said. For unnatural acts.

She's at her boyfriend's house, Grandpa said.

It felt like a fire in his head and in his chest and stomach and legs. Like a fire that was twenty feet high and twenty feet wide, and he couldn't get away from it. There were people in robes standing near the fire, in purple robes, with horns and feathers on top of their heads, and they were throwing sticks and books into the fire. And they made low moaning sounds, and they prayed, Oh God, in your goodness and in your wisdom.

And there were high trumpet and violin sounds too, and birds wheeling overhead, their wings beating the air in a rush of movement.

Gramma said, You knew about this, didn't you, little boy? From all your sneaking around? You knew every bit of it, but you thought we didn't know you knew, and you thought we'd never find out. Our little secrets. That Gramma loves her Billy boy.

Grandpa said, We didn't mean for you to be here, or for your mother to ever come here at all.

She was an orphan girl, Gramma said. No mother and father wanted her, and it made her hard and cynical and cruel. It gave her hungers and ambitions. She played with Bill the way a cat plays with a mouse.

All her years in rented rooms, Gramma said. All that time by herself. In train and bus stations. In lonely offices where she answered the telephone. Or the kitchens of restaurants, making salads, peeling potatoes, chopping onions and celery, then washing dishes afterward. And she thought if she could only catch a man in her web, could make him have his way with her, then she'd grow big with child, with her obscene issue, and it would be easy street for her.

Gramma moved the facecloth lightly over his cheeks and his neck.

That feels good, she said, doesn't it? That feels cool and nice for you.

The fire was still there, but somehow he wasn't quite so close to it. There were still people standing near the fire, but they had stopped chanting, and there were no longer any birds overhead.

Why did you go in there? Gramma asked. What did you hope to find?

Did you think you could trick us? Or escape the way your father escaped? Just like that? she asked.

Your mother is in no condition, a man said, but the man was not Grandpa or Dad.

There was a room somewhere. A room in some other place, a long time ago. A girl with dark hair and a cotton shift was sitting on the floor, playing with an empty tin can. The window was closed, its glass cracked, and outside the window was the sound of a city.

Then a woman came into the room and gestured for the girl to get up, and Jack watched her stand and go out of the room with the woman.

Gramma said, So many things could have happened to her, and so many things could happen to him or you as well.

Just think of the things, she said. All the places and possibilities.

A little boy with brown hair, she said, with freckles and blue eyes, a boy who was very small and careful and watchful, who said his prayers and snuck around and poked into things he should better have left alone—that little boy couldn't begin to understand or know.

Even though he saw things he never should have seen, she said.

Even though he himself was an accident, Gramma said. Something that crawled up out of the juice and ooze of lust and need.

Outside, the wind was blowing, and the hall light was now off, and in the dark he could barely make out faint light on her glasses. Her voice was so low and slow it was almost a whisper.

Even though he was something that never should have happened, like a bad habit or a growth or mold or disease.

She said, Even then, no matter what stories and lies he told, it still wouldn't make up for that original and deep stain of sin.

And his father would try to kill it off in the anesthetic of alcohol, and his mother would tell about her dark past, and hope in that way to cover over the stain.

Nothing worked, Gramma whispered.

Then he felt as though he was being lifted and carried, but he was pretty sure that it was only a dream. He felt wind and there was snow falling on his face.

He heard a shovel biting into dirt, and he heard chanting, and a woman said, Beautiful boy.

Come here, little boy, she said again. And it was the woman in the long black dress, the woman with the beautiful hair piled on top of her head with silver combs, and she wore a white jacket over her dress.

She said, I've been looking for you for so long.

Her voice was deep and warm and kind. Her teeth were even, and she wore earrings that were small circles of silver.

She said, I worried so much about you, and I just wanted to find you and take you home with me where we both belong.

In a white house with a white fence, and large windows that are full of sunlight. And the smell of bread baking and lilac in bloom.

No holes and no shovels.

No long echoing hallways and creaking stairs. No fires and cockroaches and no smells of boiled vegetables.

Just this tall, thin woman coming toward him because she had looked for a long time before she finally found him and now they could go home.

Because boys with freckles, with brown hair, with watchful blue eyes didn't need that much. They could keep a secret and they knew to keep their mouths shut and they knew most of the time what was good for them.

20.

HE'S A FUCKING animal, you ask me, and I don't mind in the least saying so. To do what he did and then sit in that cell all day and scribble lies into notebooks. Then sit with the priest, and never say much, just look gloomy as a hound dog. And the priest, when he's not busy molesting little boys, if you wanna know what he really does, that old faggot priest is sitting there with his rosary beads and that pile of human shit, saying God loves you and forgives you, and you can get into a robe and take out a harp and sit on a cloud in heaven, with all the other faggots and coloreds and killers. 'Cause so what if you killed your old ma and pa and grandma. At least you didn't cut them up afterward and try to eat them in a stew. Or maybe try to fuck their corpse or some such shit. 'Cause they do that nowadays. This shithole is full of them, and I know every one, down to the last sick and violent piece of shit.

You ask me and I'll tell you. You don't want to hear the facts, then don't ask me. Okay? So shut the fuck up.

Don't look at me that way 'cause I know what you're thinking. My ex-wife, she was the same way. Even my kids. They used to look at me and I know what they're thinking, and I go, Say it. Say what you got on your mind. You think I'm stupid or I don't notice. You think I'm some retard. Got a big hard boner, and the drool dribbling down the side of his mouth, and he takes a shit in his hand and starts smearing the shit all over his hair and face and chest.

Believe me. I used to work over at the Fernald School before I come here and they've got those kind of cases too. Body of a man and a big cock the size of a cucumber and a brain the size of a pea, you ask me.

But at least they were born that way or get in a crash and bash the shit out of their head. Then the Jew doctors keep them alive on machines so they can collect for all the bills, and they get some big colored women from off the boat out of Haiti or Jamaica and they feed them like a baby and wash them, then they send them over to Fernald School, and the government pays and pays.

But what do they know? They got as much brains as a log of wood. Knock knock. Nobody home up there. Never was and never will be. World without end.

So okay. So enough already. This, that, whatever. I get all worked up and I'm not as bad as I sound. Huge loud moron, with keys on his belt and a big nightstick. Keep all the assholes in line. Some of them made mistakes. Got hooked on drugs and all the shit-for-brains politicians say, Lock up the druggies and throw away the key and build more prisons and send a message and three strikes and you're out. And of course everyone yells and claps and says, Yeah, let them rot in prison, and all they are, a lot of them, are just these pitiful junkies. They just want to stay high every day. Then sit in a room and scratch themselves all day and night. Maybe listen to jazz on the radio and fuck their girlfriends or boyfriends if they can get it up. So I say, Well, Jesus, it doesn't take a rocket scientist to figure out that we just give them a prescription for their drugs and make them get a job and pay taxes. Make them into citizens, only they stay a little buzzed most of the time. Maybe their brains don't make enough of a certain chemical, so they take the drugs. So you don't let them drive or operate heavy machinery. But you give them a job and give them their hit of scag, and suddenly you empty, I'd say, half the people out of prison. And you take about eighty percent of the guns out of people's hands, and your crime problem is solved. Then they pin a medal on my chest and say, Hey, Mel, you're not as stupid as you look. You're not as dumb as you sound sometimes. And I'll tell Marleen, my ex, and the kids that. Make them come to watch the governor pin a medal on my tit. Give me a Nobel Prize for peace and I'll go with all the smart Jew scientists. King of Sweden pats me on the back, and I'll get me a big tuxedo so I look like a penguin too.

Mel Fricker. Hey, not too fucking bad. Mel's a human being. Guess what? Mel Fricker's no animal. Even though he worked all his life with the retards and scumbags, he's still got a little brain activity up there.

And I know how the coloreds and the Jews got fucked over pretty much all of human history. Put in ovens and chains and tortured and shit. I don't deny it. But they fucked over the Irish too, and you never hear about that now, do you? The boot of the Prots in the behind of the Paddies. Let me tell you about that, you want an earful.

But what can I say 'cause that scumbag Connor is a Mick too. What that tells you is assholes and pieces of shit come in all shapes and sizes and colors. Nobody has a monopoly, right. And here, they send a memo around that the Great and General Court of the Commonwealth of Massachusetts passed a bill almost ten years ago saying the state can kill these assholes, and the governor signed it. Now finally they're gonna carry one out. And they want volunteers for the execution team, they call it. Like we all put on sneakers and basketball shorts and get out needles with the drugs ready. We get in a huddle, and there's these cheerleaders and everything with pom-poms, and a game clock. Then we listen to the coach, clap our hands once, and kill the asshole. Go team go, right.

But anyway, the memo, it comes around, and all of us knew it would be Connor. And everyone's thinking too, There's no way the Commonwealth's got the balls for this. It hasn't happened since, Jesus, I don't know, maybe fifty years. Since Old Sparky, the electric chair that used to be a barber chair, I believe. And they want volunteers from the guards to take this in-service. I guess they want to teach us how to kill the motherfuckers. So first I say, Why don't they bring them out and around back near the fences, cuff the hands behind the back, make the asshole kneel down, then put the barrel of a pistol right behind the ear? Takes about two seconds and I'll let them borrow my pistol. Free of charge.

Then I think of course they're not gonna listen to me, and they're not gonna do anything sensible and cheap cause they're the government and they have to waste a lot of money and fill out a shitload of forms in triplicate and hold about fifty meetings, then have about sixty-two in-service training sessions. But I always talked how I would be happy to pull the trigger or flip the switch, only nobody ever asked me. Then I think, Okay, they finally asked me, and I said, You wanna keep flapping your jaws, you big blowhard, or you gonna have the seeds to do what you've been talking about?

So me and Calhoun, the colored guy, we're pushing the buttons. And I say, Hey, Calhoun, you just wanna be able to kill a honky motherfucker for free. This way they not only won't lynch you, they're gonna pay you extra. And Calhoun says, Fuck you, Fricker, you redneck asshole. Which is about right. So I say, Smile, Calhoun. They're gonna turn off the lights and I need to be able to see where you are, and Calhoun says, Fricker, you're a fucking Mick caveman, but he smiles. Calhoun's okay for a jig.

So they put us through all these in-services and they keep telling us how we have to do this in a real humane way and with sensitivity and the whole time I'm thinking how surprised I am that the state doesn't run these same in-services for killers before they kill, but that would probably violate their civil rights. Right?

So they get this psychologist in to talk to me and Calhoun, and guess what, his name is Goldberg or Goldman, but he turns out to be pretty much okay. Says to us that this is a job that we don't have to take, and it can be a very heavy burden to bear, psychologically speaking, especially afterwards. When you're trying to go to sleep and if you wake up alone during the night and find yourself staring into the dark, and you start thinking and mulling over things. Sometimes you'll have no appetite, Goldy says, or you'll find yourself drinking too much to forget and to get to sleep. And he asks me and Calhoun if we're married and have any kids, and we're both divorced, and I say, Hey, Calhoun, maybe we can get a place together, maybe keep each other company those lonely nights, and Calhoun, he starts laughing. He can't help it.

Goldberg wants to know what we do to relax and do we have friends and a love interest, he calls it. He probably wants to know too if I piss standing up or sitting down and how long since I last got my rocks off and such, and I think, Jeez, this could go on forever. Then there's five or six others aside from me and Calhoun. They won't push the button like us, but they'll be around Connor, and they'll be in the room at the time. Boyle the nurse will put in a needle, and this Pakistani doctor who can hardly speak the language and is blacker than Calhoun, except that his lips and nose are regular and he has straight hair, and not that kinky pubic hair all over his head. He'll be there to load the drugs into the machine. Afterwards he listens to Connor's chest to make sure his heart is stopped. Because this can't be cruel and unusual, the way the Constitution says it can't. They keep saying that in the in-service. Not that the asshole gave a shit when he snuffed his family. Cruel and unusual, my ass.

A few years ago I remember hearing on the radio about this guy in Washington State who molested little boys, then killed them with a rope around their necks. They were going to execute this dirtbag by hanging him, and then all the lawyers start saying, No, you can't hang him because that's cruel and unusual. If his neck doesn't snap in the drop when the trap door opens, then he swings and gets slowly strangled to death. It takes ten minutes to die. All the lawyers and judges say, Hey, we can't have that. That's torture. That's cruel and unusual. And then finally the dirtbag says, That's how I killed the little kids, and if I can kill them that way, then they can kill me like that. They suffered way more than I'll ever suffer, he says, and here I am thinking, Jesus H. Christ. The last honest man in America. Got his ass in a sling and he admits what a slimeball he is. So this asshole out there in Washington, this serial killer and child molester, he walks the walk. And no matter what else, you've got to admire that.

Everywhere else you go, everyone's whining and blaming somebody else. Yeah, I killed and raped and tortured people, but my father never loved me. He fucked me in the ass and smacked me around, and now that I've gotten caught fucking over everyone else and they wanna put me in the joint, I'm getting screwed again. My mother made me do it. It's not me that slit open my wife's throat. Racism made me do it, or made the cops think I did it. Go figure, you ask me.

But anyway. What. This Goldberg guy, this psychologist, he's got a big black beard like a rabbi, and these round little glasses thick as head-lights on a pickup truck. He gets me alone in this office here, over by the administration offices. Nice thick carpet and the real wood table and the water cooler with the five-gallon jug on top. Makes those glug glug sounds and the big bubbles going to the top like it's burping. He wants to know about my home life. Where I live and do I love my kids and do I get down on my knees and pray at night. And he wants to know my feelings about Connor, and if my own mother and father are still alive. I don't put it this way, but I say, I'm fifty-seven years old and I weigh three hundred and twelve pounds, and my old ma and pa been food for the worms since before my kids were born. And they're in high school now.

My blood pressure and cholesterol suck, I can hardly breathe going up stairs, and what with the blood pressure pills and the fat and such, I couldn't get it up to save my life. Even if there was some reason to get it up. Supposing some naked Playboy bunny walked into my bedroom. So it's off the map, I tell him. It's a dead issue, so to speak.

I live in a basement apartment in a complex on Route 1 in Norwood. Next to car dealers and malls. I watch the tube and I eat and I work. I don't see my kids or my ex-wife. Thank God, I guess. I pay taxes. And that's about it. Taxes and child support. So even though I know she must hate me and she's turned the kids against me, I'll wager, I send the goddamn child support every month. Always have and always will, at least until they put me in my hole in the ground and the worms start to have a feast.

Anyway, Goldberg or Goldman, he must look at me and think, Some life. Big as a fucking house and no friends. Get up, go to work, come home. Eat and eat and eat. Watch television, go to sleep in the chair, mouth hanging open. Then do it all over again. Someday pretty soon, I get the massive fucking heart attack or stroke. Face turns red, the brain shuts down, and I piss and shit my pants. Nothing happens for three or four days. Then maybe because it's summer, the body gets all swollen and starts to stink. So the old lady upstairs calls maintenance. He comes and rings the bell for five minutes. He bangs on the door. Calls on the phone from the office. Lets it ring forever. Finally he comes back and he lets himself in with the key, and as soon as he opens the door, he smells it. Sees me lying as big and bloated as a whale in my chair. And maybe the tube's still on and the sound's real low. My eyes, maybe they're still open and staring. So this guy, he thinks holy shit, and he locks the door, goes back to the office and calls the police.

I don't say any of this to Goldberg, you can bet your fat ass. I just tell him it's a job and someone has to do it, and I have no feeling one way or the other about Connor. He's just another inmate. And so forth and so on.

The priest comes back, and to tell you the truth he probably doesn't give a shit for little boys like I said. That was just spouting off. Sometimes I get carried away. This priest by the name of Curran, he's a pretty old guy himself. He must be seventy, I would say. Comes shuffling along the hall, his feet not getting much off the floor. And I let him into the room where we've brought Connor. Got a little table in there and two chairs, and they sit and the priest seems to do most of the talking. Looks down at the Bible in his hand, and has rosary beads, and it's a long fucking time since I'm around that shit.

My ma, she was always with the fathers and the saints and holy mother church all the time, not that it did her much good. Had the rosary beads her whole life, mumbling prayers under her breath all the time. And my pa, he was usually off having a drink and a laugh, then

Ma worked him over when he was with the hangover. Then maybe a week or more, Pa was on the wagon and Ma had him praying, and both of them, they had the white heads of hair and their teeth almost all gone, and they're praying and whispering, Holy Mary, Mother of God and whatnot, till the old man couldn't take it and heads out to wet his whistle. Then he's gone and Ma's always saying how he accepted Jesus God in the end, and then she's gone, and she's got the beads wrapped around in her hands, folded there in the casket.

Now Connor's got his head bent over forward, and Curran whispers shit in his ear, probably about angels and the next world. Connor's got a few gray hairs there on top, and he's got this gray skin like a mushroom. No sun in how long. Connor nods his head, then I think, Just remember what he did while his old ma and pa and grandma were asleep there in their bed. They didn't have no priest with them and no rosary beads in their hands either. And nobody asked them to pray. So you just remember that, and when the time gets here at midnight, push the button and send him on his way down to the fires.

21.

GRAMMA SAID THAT next time there would be no getting out so easily, and no whining to come back to where I thought my home and my place were, and no free ride on the welfare for the rest of my years. This time when the police came, they wouldn't be so nice and polite when they came up to the third floor, and there'd be no asking them for a smoke on the way to the hospital.

This had just gone on far too long, Gramma said, especially when you considered that I was a mistake from the very beginning, from all those years ago. I was something that had no business happening in the first place if I wanted to know the truth of the matter.

I was in her den, and I was gentle as Jesus, with all the chemicals, the pills, whispering in my bones and blood, moving all through me like clouds of ease. Just smile and nod, I kept thinking, and she pulled on the hank of yarn, and her knitting needles clicked and moved in small ovals and circles. Black yarn for a sweater for her Bill.

I'm sorry to have to tell you this, she said. I do not like causing you or anybody discomfort. But facts are facts, and I have put up with this a long, long time.

This has never been easy for me, Gramma said.

Her eyes began to fill with tears.

I've had him longer than any of you, and a mother has rights nobody else has. Rights that most people cannot even imagine. So don't try to tell me, and don't give me that quivering mouth and nostrils like you're about to cry.

She clicked her needles, and on television a car drove along a curving road, high above the ocean. The volume was so low that it sounded like more whispers coming from far away.

Gramma said, I remember carrying him all that time under my heart, and don't think that doesn't mean something.

And then when he came out, his face so red and everything covered with blood, with my blood. But then they washed him off, and he was so tiny and so perfect. He was my perfect little baby. He had ten fingers and ten toes, and perfect little fingernails and toenails.

He just looked around, his eyes all puffy and slate gray, and he looked at me, and at that moment I knew he was mine because I had made him. Not God, but me, inside my body, near my heart, and I knew that I would never, ever let anybody try to take him from me, so help me God.

Gramma said, And so the day he came home and he held onto the arm of that woman, and she held onto his arm, I knew that I would never get over this.

And then you, that awful winter day that you were born, and all you ever did was scream. Wanting everything right from the first minute, and that has never changed. Give me this and give me that.

The snow and ice fell and fell, the day you were born, Gramma said. The trees and telephone wires were all covered with ice and snow, and cars could hardly move on the roads without skidding, and you ruined Christmas for all of us that year. Coming two days before, so Bill wasn't even here with us for the holiday that year. Just up and out the door to see his whore and his unwanted, bastard child. The orphan's orphan. All of them together up at the hospital. And him risking his life, being on the road in that terrible ice and snow.

Then all the years of sneaking around and spying on us. Peeking out from under the chairs and table. Sneaking under the bed, all these years. Just weirder and weirder. Just strange and queer as a three-dollar bill. Those big eyes and the freckles on your nose that your orphan mother thought were so cute.

She was quiet for two or three minutes. She looked at me, her face tight and red. She put the needles down and sipped from a glass that was sitting on the table next to her rocking chair.

She took a ruler from her knitting basket, and measured the black patch of material she had been knitting.

You never again left us alone, except when you'd sneak off in the dark of night to prowl around. Or go off on your little trips around the country. Two, three weeks, and we'd begin to get hopeful that at long last we were rid of you. That you met your own whore somewhere, and that you'd stay with her and leave us in peace for once.

But you always came back. A week, two weeks, a month later. We'd hear your car in the driveway at three in the morning. Then your keys in the door, and your steps trudging up to the third floor.

Mother of God, Gramma said. Jesus Christ on the cross. Hovering over us like some demented angel.

Even your whore mother is terrified of what you'll do. Sneaking around, and now you're big as a football player on TV, and crazed with the pills and drink. And I can see it in your eyes. The rage and hatred. Ha, she said. You don't know the least of it.

And when they took you away, when they had you in there on the locked ward where you belong, we never should have let you back again. Kept you in there and given you shots to keep you quiet, to keep you stupid and cloudy all day and night.

Next time, they won't be so nice. Next time I tell them about your eyes and your sneaking around. Looking at the blades of knives and the lengths of rope. Thinking how we'll be sleeping and we won't even know.

And this time you'll be lying there dreaming your sick little dreams, and they'll come with their guns drawn and they'll put the barrel of the gun in your ear, in your mouth, under your chin. And they'll say, Don't even twitch. Don't even blink or breathe. You're real close to dead, they'll say to you. You're hamburger, you little piece of shit, they'll say.

And none of it will be gentle and fun anymore. Let me tell you.

Then when they put the cuffs on you, they'll roll you over and push your face into the pillow so you won't be able to breathe for a minute. And the cop's knee will be at the back of your neck, the way you deserve.

Dad sat at the kitchen table on the second floor, and sipped from a can of Pabst Blue Ribbon beer. He wore sunglasses and his overcoat, and he flipped the channels of the TV that sat on the table. He had a cigarette going, and it seemed to stick to the side of his lower lip. The smoke made him blink his eyes.

She says things, your gramma, Dad said, but she doesn't mean half of what she says. These moods come over her. They always have. Like black clouds forming over her head, then for three or four days she's dark as Hitler.

I always learned to stay out of her way because there was nothing anybody could do about it. We just learned to stay out of her way. Sometimes, especially when I was little, I'd see her sitting in the bedroom or living room, all by herself, in the middle of the day, or once in a while, real early in the morning, before it was even light out, the tears would be rolling down from her eyes. But she'd never move or make even the smallest sound. Like she was frozen under this mask, alone as an island.

But she never really meant any harm, even when she lashed out. I always knew it was her mood making her do it, and not anything she would normally do, Dad said. Even when she'd lock me in a closet for most of an afternoon, or spank me with a paddle until blood came, she'd always feel terrible. Then she'd hold me in her arms and feed me like I was a baby, or give me a warm bath, and then she'd put something on the cuts on my bottom. A balm that always made it feel better. Then for two or three days, she'd be nice as pie. Give me cookies and make my favorite dinners.

He flipped the channels fast. Thunk thunk thunk. He paused at a bobcat climbing on rocks, then flipped some more. A woman in a sparkly dress was singing.

He sipped from his can, and lit another smoke.

When we called the cops and asked them to take you to the hospital, we didn't mean for you to end up at Medfield on a locked ward. With mesh on all the windows. We figured they'd just take you to the local hospital, up to Newton-Wellesley, and they'd put you on the psycho ward for a few days. They'd adjust your meds and send you back. Get you eating again and keeping normal hours. Maybe lay off the booze a little.

You kept hearing voices, you said, and Jesus, that's scary. I don't care what anybody says.

We had to call the police. What else could we do?

It just about broke our hearts. Seeing those cops walk upstairs, big as life.

Dad said, You never think a thing like that could happen to you and your own.

A few days after they took you, I started hitting the sauce pretty hard. That's how rough it was on me. Wake up with a beer, and pretty much sip all day. Take a nap, piss the bed, wake up and keep going. Not even eat for three, four days.

Then they called and said you punched someone. Just hauled off and smashed them in the face. Broke their glasses, and they had to get something like five people in there to hold you down while they gave you a shot in the ass.

Then of course they put you in the straitjacket and dragged your ass to Medfield. Got a judge to write out a pink paper, keep you in there thirty days.

You think we were happy about all that? Dad said. You think that's what we wanted?

Your mother was crying like a baby and your grandmother just sat in her rocking chair not saying a word.

In the middle of the night one night, I got in the car and just drove. I took a handful of your mother's diet pills, the black ones, and I felt like Jesus on a fast horse for Christ's sake. The windows all down and the can of beer between my legs, and every four or five hours another pill. Smokes and booze to take down the jagged edges of the speed, and that sweet feeling like I was racing the clouds to heaven.

It's the best thing in the world while it lasts. You feel like God and his angels, and it was just white lines on the road and cars and wind, and once in a while some rain. Bugs splattering on the windshield, and trees and telephone poles to eternity. Mile after mile, and for the first few days I only stopped for gas and smokes and beer. No sleep, no shave, and no thought of you or Mom or Joanie.

Jesus H., I must of looked like something from the Bible.

Then somewhere in Nebraska, I think, everything went from green to brown, from trees to rocks, and I thought I was somewhere on the other side of the world. I was a million miles away, on the far side of Mars or something, and I ran out of whatever was pushing me on.

I'd been so jazzed up, and I'd had no food for a while, and it was just booze and pills and smokes. And I was seeing things like giant lizards and boats in the desert and men with beards and white robes standing at the side of the highway in the black of night.

I started thinking that voices were calling to me, these kids' voices saying Papa, Papa. And a woman's high voice crying like it was the end of the world, I guess.

So I pulled into this huge truck stop, somewhere near the far edge of Nebraska, I think it was. I pulled into a parking space and shut off the car, and just sat there for a while.

All around there were these huge trucks, and those bright bright lights like a prison camp or something.

I listened, Dad said. I just sat there and listened, and I couldn't hear any voices anymore.

And I thought about you being in the bin back here, and how the cops had come in, and Joanie crying and everything. And I just felt this pure rage, like ether or oxygen or God's sweet air in heaven.

I kept thinking you had no fucking right to do this to us. To your mother or to my mom or to me. I thought, Dad said, this little fucking twit had no right, in heaven and earth, to do this to us. And I thought how you were finally where you belonged.

Then everything seemed to come from farther and farther away, and sometime after that, not more than a half hour I'd guess, I fell asleep. And I had a dream that was so vivid that I remember it to this day. That I was flying over fields and rivers and lakes. Past clouds, and birds and airplanes were flying far below me. Then I was in the house in Newton and I was a little boy again. I was on the third floor, looking out the window at the end of the hall there. I could barely see over the windowsill, I was so young. Then someone came up behind me, put their arms around me and held me to their warm, tall body. And I knew from the smell of soap and flour and the softness that it was my mother. And we stood there a long time. Just the two of us. Not moving or saying anything. Just standing, forever it seemed, and the world like that was exactly perfect. It was finally right.

22.

FATHER CURRAN TOLD me a long time ago to write down everything I could remember, and that way there wouldn't be only silence and emptiness after I'm gone. He said that nothingness was the scariest thing in the world, far worse than evil or Satan. Or maybe, he said, people became evil because of the nothingness that was inside of them. Nothingness arrived because of the lack of compassion or faith or hope. He said if you never had those things and didn't really know what they were even, then Satan would appear in the absence of anything else. And then we all saw in the newspapers and on television all the time how people slaughtered other people, bombed and burned them out of their homes and churches, let children roam on the streets to be preyed upon, and saw the rich and comfortable literally step over and around the poor and homeless and destitute in our cities.

He said maybe the silence and nothingness inside each of us, the

171

despair and suffering, were part of why so much of that continues to go on and has gone on nearly forever.

He said to remember and to speak was a tiny way of working against all that. But for me most of the time, maybe sometimes only—I don't know—it seems like emptiness and nothingness are where we all have to be nearly all of our lives. It's how we were born and it's certainly how we die. It's how I will go in twelve more days. And that will be the only way out, into an even greater emptiness and silence. Into the big and final silence, I guess.

Now and then I think I should just stop, and lie here with my hands folded on my stomach, staring at the ceiling, the floor, the walls, the bars. I can feel the blood moving throughout my body, into my arms and legs, pumping from the side of my chest on its long and pointless and fruitless journey through my body. So I can rage more, hate more, remember more and more. And all the blood does is move through and around in the endless and tired work of the heart.

Or I can lie here and listen to the breath going in and out, over and over, carrying oxygen to the blood, doing more long work—so that my emptiness and hatred can go on another few weeks, days, hours, minutes, seconds. In, out, in, out, in, out. Thump thump goes my heart. But soon it will stop, and I swear, sometimes, I am mostly glad of that. To end everything. But to save the state a great deal of time and trouble, I should have done something to myself a long time ago. The same night when I did the rest. But I lacked the courage and integrity to do the right thing, the thing closest to justice. But that will be fixed soon.

Father Curran wrote down some words on a piece of paper, and I keep it with my notebooks and pencils. In case I got stuck, he said. Just try to address these questions, these words. The newspaper words, he said. Only push the questions deeper. Ask more of them.

Who?
What?
Where?
When?
Why?

How?

Then he said, Phrase it any way you want, and for a little while I thought I was back in third grade and the teacher was giving me an assignment. Use each vocabulary word in a sentence, or something like that.

A sentence, the teacher would always say.

A sentence. Right. I'll give you a sentence.

Then I thought of different sentences—and I don't mean ten years or fifty years, concurrent or consecutive or death. Or even, I sentence you to life. To live a life on this earth.

I thought of each word and then I said okay. I don't have much time, and that is how it should be, but I thought I'd try. God loves a trier, Father Curran said, and he laughed.

So for each word I make a sentence.

Who I saw.

What I did.

Where I went.

When I knew. Why I did it.

How I left.

Then Father Curran said, And think of other things. Things that didn't happen, but that might have happened if a few things had been just a little bit different.

Think hard, he said. Don't go for easy answers either. Go beyond the obvious. Sometimes, thinking about something puts that thing, that thought, into the realm of the possible. And not just bad things either. Think of good things too. Good possibilities as well.

Ways I might have been, I said.

And he said, Yes. Exactly.

If a few things, even a few small things, had been just a little bit different, Father Curran said. Any time during your life.

Maybe if I had gone left instead of right, somewhere in Ohio. Driving late at night. If I had looked up instead of down. Behind me rather than to the front. If my hair was blond or red or light brown.

Or my father didn't drink, and at night, when I was very small and lying in bed late at night, I'd think of bad things. Of monsters coming to get me. Scaled creatures with fangs. With pale yellow eyes. Or men in long coats. With candles flickering or people in hoods and long robes. And they would stand and chant, the way they had in the picture in the book that I saw, and I said, Gramma, what're they doing and she told me. Nine-nine-nine, she said. Six-six-six. Give it a little turn, a slight twist, and it's something quite other. Quite different.

But my father didn't drink. Say that that was different. He shaved every day and took a bath, and didn't sit on the couch all day, with rosary beads in his hands. Sipping from a can, saying, Hail Mary, Mother of God, pray for us sinners, now and at the hour of our death. Amen.

But say he didn't drink, and he was tall rather than short and he was happy sometimes. He took my hands in the kitchen, and he sang, Some-where, beyond the sea—and we danced and I laughed until tears came to my eyes. Say that happened, and he never sipped from cans or glasses and there were no brown bottles on the top shelves of the pantry.

So late at night, up there on the third floor, when I dreamed in the dark that monsters were coming to our house to take my toys, to take dinner away from us, to take me away to a cold and dark cave deep in the woods—my father would have been a little bit different. Taller, and he never drank.

And so, I might have been a kid who woke up from a bad dream, or who lay in bed thinking of monsters or witches or goblins in the dark, coming to get me, and I would have to get up and go down the long hall in pale moonlight, and down the creaking stairs.

The clock would be ticking in their room, and I'd see his warm, humped shape in the dark. Mom would be on her side and Dad on his side, and the numbers on the clock would glow faintly there in all the blackness.

I'd go to the bed, and he'd be on his side, facing me as I stood there. I'd put my hand on his cheek, and whisper, Dad. Then I'd pat his arm and whisper more loudly, Dad.

There would be no liquor on his breath, no sour smell of cigarettes. I'd say his name over and over, and eventually, half in sleep, he'd reach out his arm and move over to make room for me, and I'd climb into the bed. Dad would have put his arms around me, and my back would be against his chest, and he'd whisper, he'd almost mumble at first, Jack, Jack.

He'd whisper in a groggy voice, What's wrong, honey? Bad dream? Couldn't sleep? Monsters?

And I'd nod, would barely have to whisper yes, because he knew.

He was enormous and warm and he smelled like sleep. He pulled a sheet over us, and lay still for a minute or two or three.

Then he'd whisper, quiet as breath on my ear, Wanna hear a song? And I'd nod my head again.

And so soft that it was air on my skin and deep and still as night, he'd sing "Amazing Grace" and "Summertime" in a low, quavering voice. Hush, he'd whisper, empty as anything, and then we'd go a long way away, deep as, silent as, warm as sleep and the night.

23.

SO JUST BECAUSE he walked in and saw them, saw Gramma and Dad holding one another, their arms around and standing there kissing on the lips for a while, that didn't mean anything very much. That didn't mean a thing at all.

So don't say, Gramma said, and don't even think, and how dare you even think you saw something, saw what you think you saw, because it was your own filthy imagination and nothing else. So help me God, Gramma said. Sweet Jesus in heaven. Sweet baby Jesus.

Because what business, you sneak, you liar and ingrate, do you have walking around on tiptoes, and moving like a painted Indian in moccasins in the forest? Standing there as quiet as a bump on a log, and staring with your big saucer eyes, when we didn't even know, didn't even notice—and how could we?—that you were watching the whole time.

How dare you? Gramma said, and she took hold of the hair on his head with her fist. She held his hair, his head steady, then she punched him hard in the eye and nose.

She took him by the ear, twisted his arm behind his back so that his arm was pushed so high up his back that his bent hand was touching his hair at the back of his head.

You disgusting, sneaking, filthy thing, Gramma said. Little feces, she said, and she pushed him hard from the doorway into the wall on the far side of the hall.

He hit his shoulder and fell, then Gramma said, I'll teach you. I'll show you. You little. You filthy and stupid and ugly. Sneak that you are, she said.

He looked up and she squatted over him and slapped, and slapped.

Made a cracking sound, and stung, it stung like anything.

She took his hair again and lifted him by the waist of his pants and swung him at the wall.

And everything was motion, and hard, hard.

Oh, that hurt, that star, that star and everything red, and she dragged him through the hall to the kitchen, then through the door to the back hall. She opened the door, and Dad said, Mom. Mom. Please, Mom.

And she said, You cipher, you dickless piece.

Dad was crying, saying, No and No and No, and sobbing.

She opened the cellar door, and the stairs there, and the stone wall on the side above the stairs, and she said, Look down there, will you?

Spy down there, and pushed him and he went down, then it was dark and ringing, and his father said, Christ, and there were footsteps overhead.

Then not quiet, but nobody came near him, and he went over and over, slow as anything, and something wet at his head, and his arm, then something in his belly too.

And he lay there a long time and everything was black, and once after a long time he blinked, and there was light in a high window on the far side, and the furnace, and he saw a sky, he thought.

Then there were sirens and sirens, rising and falling, from far off on the other side of the world, then closer and closer.

They stopped and they stopped and a long time later, Gramma said, The door wasn't locked. The coal man must have, she said.

He fell, he's only four, almost five, and he fell, and, My God.

Please, God in heaven, Gramma said.

Our baby, and Mommy, she was crying too, and they were on the stairs. Men in blue, their radios.

One had glasses, and they had a blanket, and a long bed with handles. And, oh.

Oh, and that was stabbing his belly, and he couldn't feel his arm, it was all numb.

She bent over and whispered, You don't know. The accident, she said, was nobody's fault.

We love you so, Gramma said.

Oh, that.

His belly.

Spleen, a man said.

They lifted, and that stabbing thing that knife.

My baby, Mommy said, and Gramma sobbed and said, Beautiful beautiful boy, we love so much. We adore, we would give our lives for him.

Everything swirled and spun and the sky up there, and they slid him in, and there were small cabinets and things hanging on the side, tubes and bottles and a strap at his knees, his shoulders, and a man with glasses, in blue, on a stool near his head.

Said, Okay, you're on the way, we'll fix you up.

We'll take you where they'll fix you all up, the man said.

Bad fall and hurt, he said, and the siren, it was loud as the car horn, it hurt his ears, he wanted to cover his ears but couldn't.

Out the window the world began to move fast, as fast as anything.

Wires, trees, the tops of houses went by.

And his belly, oh, his arm and his head.

Numb, but then a stab, then tingly. Then pins and needles all over. That pinch on his arm, but numb too.

The tops of houses raced by, and the siren didn't hurt his ears so much when they moved so fast. Around a corner, and streetlights out there and up high.

For a long time they went as fast as a rocket in a book, and he was pretty sure he was spinning around, and stars and moons were whirling past him.

They lifted him, and they said, Jack. They said, Little boy.

Giants way up there. Lady and men giants, standing high over him, and moving down halls, and long tubes of light in the sky, but no stars anymore, just pinholes in squares in the ceiling.

Sweet boy, they said.

Poor pumpkin, a woman said.

Poor hurt possum, she said, and she was an angel in white, with glasses and a halo of hair. Far up there.

Jackie, they said. Jackie, can you hear me? a man said. A man with a crewcut and tubes coming out of his ears.

There was something cold on his chest and a bump on his knee and his leg kicked without even trying to.

Something warm and wet at his head, something that smelled like soap.

Then another pinch at his arm. A lady with a white hat, a funny white box of a hat on her head, she said you'll feel a pinch, but the pinch was already over when she said it.

Then a burning in your arm, she said. It'll feel hot, but just for a second, and then, she said, then, she said, then, she said again and again, and from far away, and then loud and then in a whisper.

And he was whirling far away in cold and dark and distant space, and he was pins and needles, and cool and warm at the same time.

This was sweet and gentle, and Jesus would smile when he saw me, Jack thought, and there was music, soft music in the room or in space.

Someone with scissors was cutting his clothes away from his body, and saying, The arm.

Was saying, Sutures, which was something he needed, they said.

Hold still, she said, a woman with a soft voice somewhere said.

Now, she whispered, a pinch, then a little pull.

Sometime later, he thought it must be ten miles later and hours and hours away, he was blinking, and there were blip sounds. Blip, blip, then ping, ping, like a spaceship, like something turning slowly in the darkness.

They put a damp warm cloth on his forehead, and wavering voices, miles and years away, said, Hey, little boy.

Sweet little boy, they whispered, soft as a cotton ball, a cold cotton ball on the inside of his arm. Then they said, Pinch, this'll pinch, then hot, then all done, all better almost.

You'll be up in no time, only soon, she said, in a day or two, we'll take you to the special room and we'll put you to sleep and we'll fix you inside too so your belly won't hurt, won't sting and burn and bleed in there.

Gramma was next to his ear, and she said, You had dreams, you thought they were real. You had dreams, and you moved around in the dark, and you thought you saw things.

Crazy things, Gramma whispered.

Nobody would ever believe you, she said. They wouldn't think a word of it was true.

Very very late at night, and you thought you were walking around, seeing things and hearing things.

The night is tricky, Gramma said. The dark tells lies.

Then it was later, but he wasn't sure how much later. Then Dad said something. He said he was very sorry to see his little boy hurt so much, and to be lying there with tubes in his nose and the back of his hand, and everywhere else too. Places he didn't want to mention.

So sad and such a bad accident. And for nothing too. Because that man, that cleaning man or that coal man or the man who looked at the furnace—one of them had left the door unlocked, and look what happened and all for no reason.

Dad's breath smelled like mint and medicine, and his words were loose and slurry. His tongue was off a little bit.

Dad sat in a chair next to the bed and leaned forward, and his head was down like he was praying. He pressed the top of his head against Jack's upper arm and at his shoulder, and he shook a little with crying, and tears fell on Jack's arm and hand.

Your gramma doesn't mean it, Dad said. She's nice most of the time.

She makes cookies and bakes cakes. She cleans house and knits and sews. Everybody who knows her loves her. She's a very good woman most of the time.

She just goes off once in a while, Dad said. The moon comes out and bats fly in the dark outside, and she gets all closed in and hot and angry as a burning frying pan. Put water on it and it spits at you. It'll burn you bad.

So you learn to stay away. Just don't go near because you'll get hurt, and it's not really her fault. She can't help it, I think.

People in white went past in the hall, their shoes scuffing the linoleum. They carried trays or pushed carts or wheelchairs. The people in wheelchairs had white hair and gray skin. Their mouths hung open.

Dad said she had always been like that, as far back as he could remember. Nice and smiling, all hugs and kisses and little jokes and things, then the hurricane came in and her face was dark as thunder, as quick and angry as lightning.

So you had to go and hide somewhere, maybe in a closet, behind coats or boxes, and peek out and see her go by in the hall. Furious and mad and just filled with hurt and hate.

Maybe you could go under the bed or up in an attic or tree. Maybe to the cellar. Hide down there, under the stairs. With paint cans and dusty, greasy tools. Hear the furnace come on like a big animal waking up.

Her mother and father came from the old country, came from Sweden a long, long time ago. Before she was even born.

Gramma's father had a mustache and a soft quiet voice, and he was nice as pie, nice as the day is long. Smiled, and had a gentle quiet way about him. Go to work, come home, kiss his wife and his little girl, then sit in the living room and read the paper, smoke a long brown cigar that smelled like burning leaves in late October.

Dad said he remembered Granddad, all that time ago. Very quiet and calm. Very gentle.

But the mother, Dad said, Grandma Lundquist, she was something else too. Someone you had to be careful with. Someone you had to tiptoe around.

Big strong arms and a chin, and a voice like a banging hammer.

Boom, boom, boom, boom, boom.

Come over here.

Hey, you.

I'm your mother, she said, and the glass in the windows trembled at her voice.

I'm your mother, I'm your grandmother, and don't you ever forget it, little Miss High and Mighty, little Mr. So and So. And she took you by the ear or by a pinch of skin on the arm or shoulder. Twisted it and said, you fuss and I'll really give you something to cry about. You think this hurts, you have another thing coming to you and I can tell you now that you won't like it.

Then we ran and hid. Under the porch and in bushes, and my mom, Dad said, my mom when she told me would start to cry and hold me, and stroke the wet tears on my face. Said, Beautiful little boy. Beautiful boy. My prize. My gift. My child. My joy.

Then Dad was silent, and kept his head on Jack's arm, and sometime later someone said—a nurse said, Jack thought—said, Mr. Connor, Jack, Mr. Connor, and Dad lifted his head and mumbled as though he had been sleeping. Then Dad kissed Jack's forehead, on the hair there, and said, So long.

He got up and moved slowly out of the room.

The nurse smiled and said, You okay? You feeling relaxed? Any better at all?

She wanted to know if his belly still hurt, and he said he wasn't sure, he really couldn't tell.

She said, I can get you more medicine, and moved the back of her hand slowly on his cheek. Up, down, up, down.

Then she left, came back, touched a cold spot on his upper arm. He felt a pinch, then he just lay there as quiet and still as a piece of wood. Air moving around over him and bats flitting past the eaves of some dark barn.

High above him, the sky was mostly dark but with a streak of deep blue and pink at the upper rim of the sky. And birds were outlined against the pink. Gramma, somehow, was next to him and she was floating in air just as he was. Only she was a little girl, except that she had big strong hands like an old mean lady.

She smiled at him, then Gramma's mother was passing at a distance, scowling, and she looked up and down, she looked over her shoulder on each side, but she didn't see them.

Then Mom kissed Jack's head where the bandage was, but it didn't hurt. It was light as a breeze.

Come with me, Momma said. To when I was as little as you.

And they were walking slowly through an enormous room, full of little children in white who had no mother or father. They all had dark eyes and pale skin. They were beyond sad, and Jack and Momma tried to reach out to them, tried to say things. To say, Don't worry. Say, We love you. Say, Nobody will hurt you. But there was a thick sheet of glass between him and Momma, and the orphan children.

Then the orphans turned away and began to file through a single doorway on the far wall. A tall nun in a long black habit stood at the doorway, and checked off names on a clipboard. She had glasses with metal frames, and her eyes were very small.

Momma said, That's me, the one going in. When he looked, she had already gone through the doorway into the darkness beyond.

And when he turned back and looked on his side of the glass, his mother was also gone.

Little boy, strange voices said softly to him. Little little boy.

He was still and silent, and there were pins and needles all over his body, but they didn't hurt. They felt funny but good, and the top of his head felt very cold.

What a sad accident, Gramma whispered, and she pinched a fold of skin on his side. But it didn't hurt.

How sad and tired, she whispered, and what strange dreams you've had.

Then Dad said, She loves me too much. She loves me more than all the world. She won't let anyone else near. Not ever, so go away.

Gramma said she felt bad to do such things, even in dreams. Even in his sick and deviant imagination.

She said that late at night, when the world was dark and you didn't know if you were asleep or awake, and if something was real or a dream, it was hard to tell anything or know anything.

Who could say what was true? Gramma said.

Then Momma and Dad, Gramma and even Grandpa, who seemed to have gone somewhere for a while, they gathered together over him in robes, scarlet robes and sea-green robes, with stars and half-moons on them, and they hummed very softly.

That they loved him and that he would sleep for a long time. That soon this would be over. Then he would wake up again and again, and sometime, somewhere, there would be something like peace.

24.

I THINK OF my own ma and pa when they were quite old. Their heads were white, their hands were spotted brown with age and shook with all the years. They had thin hair on their pink skulls, fine as the lace curtains Ma hung in the living room and kitchen. When I looked at them, I always thought of a baby's skull, before the bones of the head knit together. They seemed overall to be fragile as a baby too. Ma and Pa. In their late seventies, and Ma turning eighty finally. They were both pretty shaky on their pins, and even as they raised a cup of tea to their lips, the hands shook and spilled a little tea, and they pursed their lips like they were sucking lemons. It was pretty sad to see, but almost a little comical too, I'm embarrassed to admit.

I always thought Pa would be one of those difficult old men, after his retirement from the water department here in Newton. One of those old guys with too much time on his hands. He wouldn't shave for three or four days in a row. He would wear an old bathrobe around the house with soup stains down the front. Black socks and slippers, and the white hairless legs showing between where the socks ended and the bathrobe began. His hair all mussed, and him going to the front door to wave a stick at kids walking on the front lawn.

Hey, you kids, get the hell off the lawn before I call the cops, I always imagined him saying. And the kids, of course, like most kids anywhere, would laugh and give him the finger.

We get calls at the station every day or two from people like that, saying the kids are on the lawn, or stepping on the flowers, or leaving candy wrappers or empty cigarette packs on the front walk or the drive-way. Damn kids, they say. What the hell is wrong with kids these days?

They always think the kids are out of control and nothing like kids used to be. But that's an old man's prerogative, I think. It comes with the territory, like *Reader's Digest*, visits to the doctor and having to get up to pee at least twice during the night.

As it turned out, Pa wasn't like that at all. For the first few years of his retirement, when he had the energy, he used to volunteer to teach reading in the grammar school, and the neighborhood kids seemed to love the old guy. They'd shovel the walk or mow the lawn, and he'd always get them to come in for a hot chocolate or a lemonade. They'd sit at the kitchen table while Pa paid them and Ma put some cookies—always gingersnaps—on a little plate on the table. Pa asked how their sisters and brothers were, and what their best subject in school was, and what their favorite books and movies were.

Anyway, who can ever tell how somebody will end up? Thirty years earlier he was a tough Mick, a bantam who was always quick to tell you how the poor old Paddies were persecuted by the English and then, after they got starved out of Ireland, how they were persecuted by the Yankees here in Boston. But then the Paddies took over. The fire, the police, the street and water departments, then City Hall. Mayor Fitzgerald, President Kennedy's grandpa, Mayors Curley, Collins, White, Flynn, and back and forth over the years. Speakers of the House, John McCormick, and Tip O'Neill, who Pa met on numerous occasions, he'd tell you, and Tip always remembered Pa's name, even though Pa had moved to Newton years earlier.

But never mind all that. He and Ma raised me and my sister Emma Rose, and went to church, and they did their best for us. Sending us to the nuns for school, and making sure we stayed the hell out of trouble and did our homework. Finally they sent us to the fathers over at Boston College, where Tip himself had gone, and maybe that's why they were so serene those last years. Everything they hoped for their kids, or almost everything, worked out. Emma Rose is with the postal administration, and I made detective only seven years after getting on the force. If it wasn't for the time in Vietnam, I would have been under thirty when I finally got my detective's badge. Ma and Pa, let me tell you, were very proud of their fair-haired boy.

Not that there weren't bumps on the road, or pretty serious problems along the way. Emma's husband Kevin with the booze, then the divorce, and God knows it's not always been easy between me and Kirsten.

But I didn't mean to go on so. Life is like that, and people always say, you take the good with the bad, and when you get married you say it's for better or worse, and that's what you do. What choice is there really? Put one foot in front of the other, and go on.

So when it happened, when the call came in early that Sunday morning, I was home sleeping. Maybe it was two, maybe two-thirty. They beeped me, and I remember how hard it was to shake off the sleep, and pick up the phone. Like there was this great heaviness over me, and just moving an arm or leg seemed like terrible hard work.

I was on call with Raymond Petrino, who's also a good friend, and that made it easier to roll out. Because I always trusted him, and I knew if I showed up half asleep, he'd watch my back.

The dispatcher said it was on Clifton, and she said it was a possible homicide, and that'll get the blood in your veins moving like nothing else will. By then I think it was pushing maybe three in the morning, and the streets were almost completely deserted, of course. They would be by then, even on the Saturday-Sunday overnight.

When I got to Clifton, I could see the cruiser lights a quarter mile down the street, the blue-red, blue-red flashing around and around and around, and there were three cruisers out front, I recall. I knew right away that this one was very hot because the three of them wouldn't have stayed otherwise.

I pulled up across the street and went up to the front porch of this two-family, and went in the first-floor apartment. They had Connor cuffed already. He looked like an individual who had not slept, eaten, or bathed in quite some time. He was on a chair at the dining room table, and already I could detect the stink. This was August, that hot, hot summer of 1988, and we didn't know for sure at the time—of course we couldn't know—but the bodies had been there a solid week.

This smell wasn't new to me, naturally, in this line of work, but when I went past the dining room and into the kitchen, it got worse. I put a handkerchief over my nose and mouth, and one of the officers who followed me in from outside, a big good-looking guy named Kenney, said, She's in the bedroom in back.

I went into the hall off the kitchen, went left, then into the bedroom. The grandmother was lying in the bed, in a nightgown, with her hands folded on her stomach, holding rosary beads, the same as you'd see on a corpse laid out in a funeral home. The only strange thing, I remember, was that there was a white cloth the size of a handkerchief covering her face.

Even with the cloth, you could see she was very old, and that she'd been dead at least a few days. The body was beginning to turn dark with the blood settling and the decay. And the smell, God knows, was pretty bad. Leave a few pounds of raw hamburger in a closed house for a week in the summer, say, and you'll have an idea, a fraction of a sense, of the smell.

Other than that, the scene looked pretty peaceful, almost as though she had died a natural death.

Kenney, the officer with me, said, He says he did her a while ago, maybe six or seven days ago. And he says the mother and father are upstairs. This one's the grandmother.

Anyone been up there? I asked. Kenney said, Negative.

Back in the dining room, John Connor, the son and grandson, was still sitting, his cuffed hands resting on the table. He didn't appear too good himself, if you want to know the truth.

Even sitting down, he was a big fellow who looked like he'd been through something. He watched me for a little time, then he turned away. I stood on the far side of the table and said, I'm Wade Christie. I'm a lieutenant with the Newton police.

He stared at me when I said this, and I reached my hand over the table and shook his cuffed right hand.

What's your name? I said.

Real quiet and steady, he said, John Connor, and I had this strange feeling right there that the name would be known all over metropolitan Boston and New England by the Monday-morning edition of the *Globe*. Front page, plus lead story on all the TV news stations.

You want to tell me anything? I said, and after ten or twenty seconds, he shook his head.

Is that your grandmother in there? I asked him, and right away, he nodded slowly.

Then I asked Officer Kenney if Connor had been placed under arrest, and if he'd had his rights read to him. I wanted to assume that he had because of the cuffs, but you can't tell all the time.

Kenney said, Yes, and I turned to Connor and asked him if that was right, if he should have been placed under arrest.

He nodded again.

Petrino came in then, and I indicated with my head toward the back room, and heard Petrino going down the hall.

I just stood there a minute or two, then Petrino came into the dining room, looked at Connor and said, You did that to her? And Connor nodded.

Asshole, Petrino said. Fucking asshole.

Ray, I said, and he looked over, then I looked at Kenney. You want to get backup and crime-scene people here? I said, and he started out.

And don't let anyone else in until they get here, and he said, Check, like it was a detective show on television.

You live here, asshole? Petrino asked, and Connor didn't look up.

John, I said, make it easier on everybody.

Talk to me, John, I said.

Fuck the little asshole, Ray said. Put him in the joint and they'll line up to fuck the little bastard in the ass till there's blood and come dripping out of his asshole. Then they'll line up again, and the next day, and the day after that, and all the bloods and the Aryan scumbuckets will take their turns fucking him, and then he'll get AIDS, which is better than he deserves.

Ray, I said, easy, would you?

Connor still didn't look up, but we sort of knew he was listening. All of this was for him.

Work with me, John, I said. Ray gets way too pissed way too fast.

Officer Kenney came back and said backup and scene people were on their way.

Mom and Dad upstairs? I asked Connor, and he said, Yes. The second floor.

Kenney stayed with Connor, and Ray and me went through the kitchen to the hall in back, then up the stairs. The plaster in the walls was cracked, and the stairs creaked. The smell, which had been less strong in the hall and on the stairs, got bad again on the second floor.

We couldn't find the light switches at first, so we used flashlights. I think I'll always remember what that looked and felt like. The red and blue flashers still going on the cruisers out front, and lighting up patches of walls and ceiling and doorways there on the second floor. And Ray and me with our circles of light bouncing on the walls. And more cars outside on the street, because the media was always monitoring police calls. Then the stink, and how weird the place was. Stacks of papers and dishes and empty cups and glasses and bottles all over the place.

On the table and stove and washing machine in the kitchen, then on the table and chairs in the dining room too.

There was one lamp in the living room, but when I tried to turn it on, it didn't work.

When we went into the hall, both of us had handkerchiefs over our faces, so we must have looked like bandits. And both of them, the mother and father, were lying on the bed in their bedroom. And same as the grandmother, they were carefully arranged on their backs, with their hands folded and holding rosary beads and resting on their stomachs. Then the weird thing—they both had white cloths over their faces, and we later found out the cloths were a pair of the grandmother's underpants on each face.

Go figure. Like he didn't want them to see what he had done.

We didn't know any of this at the time, and we weren't even sure that these people were a father, mother, and grandmother to Connor. But the more we looked around, the sadder and stranger things became.

There was a back bedroom, for example, directly over the grandmother's bedroom. It was piled with junk, like the rest of the apartment. There was an old china cabinet with glass doors in front, and all the cups and saucers and little dishes inside were covered with maybe a half inch of dust. There was a rack for drying clothes with socks and undergarments and T-shirts hanging on it, and a sagging couch against one wall. The couch had no legs—they had been sawed off—and so it rested close to the floor.

There was also a small desk with what looked like an old living room lamp on it. This lamp worked, and when I turned it on, I saw books on prayer, on meditation, on grief and cancer and loss. There were pop psychology books about feeling okay, and bad things happening, and one on the Greek philosopher Aristotle.

I checked the drawers, and found one with five or six pairs of eyeglasses. There were paper clips and blank notebooks, and pens, a ruler, and empty envelopes in the other drawers. And rosary beads and small cards with a picture of Jesus on one side and prayers on the other side. One prayer, I recall, started something like, Lord, make me an instrument of thy peace.

There was a single light socket in the middle of the ceiling. But instead of a lightbulb, a brown extension cord ran from the light socket, across the ceiling, then down a corner of the wall. That's where the lamp on the desk was plugged in.

I remember, too, even though this was almost ten years ago, that the radiator next to a closet door had white paint on it, and that at least half the paint was chipped off, and underneath was a dark, rusty brown color. And under one end of the radiator, where a shut-off valve was, there was an empty plastic container, an old quart-size ice cream container, I would guess, that was supposed to catch water leaking from the radiator.

Ray Petrino had gone back downstairs to get the crime-scene people up to photograph and dust and measure everything. That's when I went back out in the hall at the top of the stairs. There was another door on the right, and when I turned the handle, it was unlocked, and there were stairs going up.

This was maybe four-thirty or five in the morning, and I went up slowly. I only used the flashlight, because when I got to the hall at the top of the stairs, there seemed to be moonlight coming in the windows.

There were only three rooms up there, but it couldn't have been more different than the second floor. Everything was neat and dusted. A pair of shoes and a pair of sneakers were lined up in the closet, and cups and dishes were washed and stacked in a kitchen cabinet. There was a front room that was used for a living room. There were a bunch of true-crime books stacked neatly on bookshelves, and a desk where all the pens and pencils were lined up.

The only strange thing, aside from this tight feeling of neatness, was that the windows were all closed and locked, and the cord from a telephone that was sitting on a table had been unplugged from the wall, and the cord was wrapped neatly around the phone.

I walked back to the kitchen and saw some empty liquor bottles lined up on the floor near the small kitchen table, and prescription pill containers—and there were quite a number of them—were arranged on a counter like a row of soldiers.

At the window at the end of the hall, by the top of the stairs, I looked out, and I could see a long way. And off against the dark gray sky, I could see the steeple of Our Lady's Church, where I'd gone with Ma and Pa when I was a squirt. Ma and Pa, at the time, hadn't been gone more than ten years. And here I was on another Sunday morning, standing there and looking out. And I couldn't think of the last time I had even been near a church.

25.

MOM SAID SHE had tried for as long as a person could try, and she had put up with as much as any normal person could put up with, and she couldn't do this much longer. She said she knew she had said this before, over and over, but this time she was serious. This time she meant business.

I'm surrounded by weirdness, she said. Weirdness underneath me in the form of your grandmother, your father's weirdness next to me when I sleep, and most of all, weirdness over my head. Walking up and down and up and down like some sword hanging by a piece of thread.

You think we don't know, Mom said. You think we don't see it in your eyes.

Jesus Christ on a bicycle, she said. Jesus H. Christ in a racing car or driving a garbage truck, for all I care. Rising out of his grave Easter morning and whoop de doo. Big fucking deal.

And I don't mean any disrespect to the Lord, Mom said.

Dad was in the back room at his desk. Looking at the top of the garage, at the clotheslines, at the roofs of houses, at the leaves in all the trees.

Mom looked very old, but not as old as Gramma. Mom had lines in her face, and everything about her sagged. Her eyes were pale blue, with yellow and red mixed in.

She said they had done all they could for me, and it was now up to me to get going and get on with life. She couldn't just sit there and let this go on and on, until something terrible happened.

I have dreams, she said. Mom said. Joanie said.

Dreams that you're moving through the house and that you have cans of gasoline and you're spreading it all over the first floor and second floor of the house. You're smiling that strange little smile of yours.

You're splashing the gasoline all over, especially at the front and back doors, and in the hallways, and you're opening windows so oxygen can get in, and it's late when you do this. It's got to be midnight, and in the dream, we're all asleep, even though I can watch you and sleep at the same time.

I can watch, Joanie said, but I can't do anything or say anything. I'm frozen in sleep.

Then you reach in a pocket and you light a match, and there's an explosion of flames. And you walk through the flames with your smile— and that's when I know that you're the devil. Some years ago, when none of us were looking, you went over to the other side.

Every time, though, I wake up and I feel you upstairs there, and I can't even tell what's worse anymore—the dream or you being upstairs.

Mom said it wasn't always like this, that I wasn't always so strange and locked in, so weird and secretive.

She said, You used to be almost normal, when you were just a little boy. You screamed a lot of the time, and you always wanted to be held, and we tried to do that. But it kept on, the screaming and the tantrums, and then we let you scream yourself to sleep. And that could go on for hours. You don't know the kind of torture that could be. That unreasoning infliction of pain.

We almost put a sock in your mouth, on more than one occasion. I swear to God we did.

But your grandmother said not to. She said, What're you? Crazy?

And you don't know that, Mom said. All she did for you. No matter what else you say about her. Held you and rocked you. Woke up at all hours to see that you were all right.

Now it's all lies. Lies all the time. Morning, noon, and night. Poor brave Jack, Mom said. Poor pitiful brave Jack.

They did this to me, Joanie said in her little girl's voice. They did this and they did that. They locked me in the closet and they made me sleep in the cellar and they burned me with cigarettes and they never hugged me.

Mom said, All lies. As though we didn't have enough trouble before you came along. As though we didn't already have enough to do. Your father off somewhere and keeping up with the house. Your grandmother's moods.

God help me, Mom said. It was never one bit easy.

Come from nowhere, Mom said. Everyone laughing and saying things to me. Words like lashes. Words that sting and burn and don't ever go away.

Sticks and stones, she said. Ha ha.

What a big fat lie. What a big fat ugly lie.

Names hurt. They scar you and cripple you, Joanie said. They leave you bleeding.

Sure it wasn't perfect, but who ever promised perfect? You want a nice childhood, you want love. I'll give you love with a slap in the face. With spit in your eyes. Gum in your hair. Push you in a mud puddle. Put snow down your underwear. Nobody loves you. Nobody wants you, Mom said.

Never did want you. Never will.

Joanie said, Leave you on a doorstep like a stray puppy. Leave you in the woods to die. On the side of a mountain.

Nobody knows or cares.

You think there's enough to go around? Think again, stinky. Stupid. Ugly.

She just looked down, and for a long time breathed slowly. She refolded her hands once, then she said, I hate her more than I hate all the world. Your grandmother. And she hates me just as much.

But your father loves her as much as I hate her, and she loves him as much as she hates me.

There's no other room, Mom said, so forget your lies and all the rest of it.

No more stories or anything, she said.

The cops, when they come again, they get a pink paper to keep you on the ward thirty days, Joanie said. We get a court order preventing you from coming here again.

Thirty, forty years, Mom said. That's just about enough.

You get yourself a job, a room to live in. Maybe save a little money. Maybe someday, you get a girlfriend who's just like you. She's a little fat, a little ugly, maybe a little slow upstairs.

Maybe she says her old man raped her, fucked her when she was ten years old. Maybe fucked her in the asshole. Got his drunk asshole buddies in to fuck her too. So boo hoo.

She cries on your shoulder, you cry on her shoulder.

You get a room together, lots of cockroaches crawling around, and you have a job in some sheltered workshop. Put peanuts in plastic bags all day, get a blue star at the end of the day. Get a soda at lunch together. Eat Devil Dogs and Twinkies, take your Haldol and Prozac together.

You don't like that, you think you're pretty smart for that, but you're just like them. Wearing funny clothes, waiting for the short bus to come and take you back to the home or the hospital. Hear voices. Not knowing enough to wipe yourself. So you smell like shit all the time. But your fat girlfriend, she doesn't notice or care. She smells like shit too.

The happy couple, Mom said.

. . .

Dad said they might drive there at night and they might have four or five or six of them this time, because this would be the last time, and they knew I might try to fight like hell. Big oaf like me could put up quite a fight.

He'd seen it himself, the few times he was in 'cause of the booze and pills, and then hearing voices and trying to drink lighter fluid.

How they got all around you and brought you down to the floor, and tried to hold you down for the straitjacket and the shot. It was unbelievable how a person could fight and swing, scratch and bite, scream, squeal, kick, piss and spit, all at the same time. And he'd seen one wiry guy, couldn't have been more than one-sixty, one-seventy, but pretty tall. Must have taken seven or eight people to get him down. Big people too. People trained in this shit, and he was still screaming, foaming at the mouth—but they got the asshole. They put him right down, and shot his ass full of Haldol or Prolixin—one of those drugs would stop a charging, pissed-off rhino.

Or use Mace if they had to.

Make your face and your eyes burn, your mouth and nose. Itch and burn like there was no tomorrow.

For me, Dad said, for me it wasn't so bad because I knew I had to go in for my own protection. Couldn't be outside in the world. Falling asleep at the edge of a creek, face an inch or two from the water. Fall asleep on train tracks, at the edge of a highway, legs right on top of the yellow line, just past a sharp curve, so a driver couldn't see you there.

Believe me, Dad said, Bill said. It happened all the time and he knew how that felt, to wake up with the cigarette burns on your fingers, burns on your chest and arms, and you didn't even feel it. Was so drunk, so fucked up and numb on pills and booze that they could have put you on a table and taken out your kidney, your lung, one of your legs, and you wouldn't feel it, know it, have any idea whatsoever.

That's what you got for looking for bliss, for a little peace or just a break from the hurt. You got worse and worse. You poured wood and gasoline on the fire, and it got bigger of course.

But let me tell you, he said. It was all right here, Bill said, and he tapped the left side of his chest, he tapped the side of his head.

Inside, where I had never thought to look. In my heart and mind and soul.

He looked at me and said, Will you pray to Jesus with me, son? Will you ask our Lord for help?

Because your mother and grandmother, they can't take this anymore, Dad said.

This will be the last time. The last bet, the last card face up on the table, and you've already played it and your pockets are empty, son, and we know it.

You're a drug addict and an alcoholic and a mental case, and you're as full of hate as anyone I've ever seen in my life—inside or outside the walls of any state hospital or prison.

Bill said, If you could offer it up, just give it over to Jesus, and let him take care of everything.

He's watching us now, Dad said.

He said, I know how you feel, and I don't blame you.

You have every reason.

You were so small.

Too young to know what you were getting into.

You had freckles on your nose and soft hair.

Very smooth clear skin. Like a clean pillowcase, fresh off the clothesline.

Blue eyes, Dad said. An October sky.

Beautiful eyes.

I remember, Bill said, how the moisture gathered in your eyes like a clear film, even as we watched, the four of us, and the film thickened and the tears came.

Fell down your cheeks, and your face just riven by pain.

At maybe three, three and a half years old.

It was hard to watch, Dad said.

None of us wanted it to be like that, Bill said.

You didn't get to be ninety-two, Gramma said, without remembering one thing or another. That was one hell of a long time, if I do say so, she said.

You'd have to be a pinhead or a retard not to pick up a few things along the way. And believe me, Belle said. I have.

Once, a long, long time ago, when she was a little girl herself, there was a fair that came to town and set up in a park, and she went with her daddy. Inside a tent, when it was dark outside and all the colored lights were on and were very bright. But they went inside and there were booths. There was a man in a cage who had hair all over his body and walked on his legs and on the knuckles of his hands. There was a dead baby in a big jar, and the baby floated in some liquid and had two heads, and there was a live pinhead, a lady who wasn't very old, and the top of her head was like an ice cream cone turned upside down. She sat on a stool and drooled, and there was a look in her eyes the same as the eyes of her dolls at home. Just glass and empty and silent as the world at night.

Let me tell you, Gramma said. I have seen a thing or two and I remember, and even when my momma got mad, when she sat in her rocking chair like a boiling pot on the stove, I knew when to hide under the bed or in the closet, and sometimes under the porch out back.

Her brother William, why he was never very normal, Belle said. He had white white skin like a ghost, and nervous eyes as big as the floating heads of that baby in the tent.

Daddy said William was touched by God in a special way, and when he was old enough to talk, he said things in a funny way.

William said, Applesauce, table, bird don't fly.

He called me Broom girl, she said, and when you went too close to him, he would scream and rave, as though you were about to hit him with a stick or whip him with a leather belt on his bottom.

Gramma said that at ninety-two, God was supposed to be close at hand, with his angels and the music floating up there in some great roofless house.

She could hear wings faintly fluttering and beating the air softly, and whisperings that she couldn't make out, but she didn't suppose it was anything that mattered or made any kind of difference. Not at this stage, and not if she lived to be one hundred years old, which would be some accomplishment. But she doubted she'd ever get there, and who would care one way or the other?

At her age, her bones hurt and her knees and shoulders and elbows, and there was some kind of buzz or hum in her ears, off and on, but almost all the time too.

Belle said, I'm too old to give a damn one way or the other, and she smiled, and her false teeth were perfect and even and white.

I'm supposed to think of God all the time, she said, but who the hell was he, after all? He made people suffer and starve. He made people cruel, and if he did exist after everything was said and done, and she very much doubted he did, then he had a very great deal to answer for, like every other man in power she'd ever heard of.

Like William, she said, and his screams in the middle of the night, and it was like sticking needles in Momma to see what the scream did to her.

Then they took him away to a special place, Belle said, somewhere far out in the country, on a hill, with a view of a lake and of hills and flowers, and he would be very happy there, it sounded so much like heaven.

Momma said sometimes, when I didn't listen and do as I was told, that I would go to the special place where William had gone. Only it wouldn't be quite as nice because I had a choice to go there or not, based on my behavior, and William didn't have a choice.

So late at night, when so many secret things happened, they'd come for her. In tall black coats and with horses and a carriage outside and it would be raining hard the whole way there.

Gramma would never see her brother William either, even though Momma said they would visit him. After a year or two, and William getting used to his surroundings still, he was very happy with the care and love in the special place, Momma said. Then one night, when nobody was looking, water came in and filled William's lungs so he couldn't breathe, and that was the end of him. Just like that. His eyes floating in water forever, like the special baby in the jar.

26.

THE TIME THEY had lemon sherbet on the front porch and watched the cars go by on Clifton Street out front. That was nice.

Gramma and Grandpa sat in green rocking chairs, Dad sat on the porch railing, Mom sat on the front steps, and he sat on the other side of the porch, on the floor, his back against the wooden slats of the railing. The sherbet was cool and he felt it melt slowly on his tongue, and after a while, Grandpa looked over at him and said, That's good sherbet you're eating. We paid good money for that sherbet.

He nodded, then everyone turned away and watched the red taillights of cars fade in the darkening evening. And after a while longer it was even more dark, and nobody said or did anything else that night. Just listened to crickets making their sounds and watched cars and felt breezes so slow and warm they couldn't even move the leaves on the trees.

Lying in bed in the winter, sometimes, up on the third floor, he thought they were so tired downstairs, and they had been drinking so long—since lunch maybe—that none of them would come all the way to the third floor to say or do anything.

So he just lay there, and once or twice he got out of bed, and knelt in front of the window, and looked at the patterns of ice on the window, which looked to him like cutouts of snowflakes, only smaller and more intricate. He used his hand to make a space in the ice to see out of, and there were bare branches with snow on them outside. There were rooftops with snow, and he could feel cold air at his feet and ankles and running up his legs.

So he got back in bed and imagined the cold stars shining in the freezing air, and beyond that, God in heaven, who loved him. God in a white beard and a white robe, and Mother Mary sitting next to him on a gold throne, and both of them watching on a giant movie screen. Watching him, John Connor, lying in bed and not sleeping. And thinking of them, God and Mother Mary, and Jesus too, somewhere, watching out for him.

They were watching and they knew everything. So that was nice for him too.

It was nice how Dad, once in a while, when he had just opened a new bottle—and so it was still mostly full—it was nice then how happy he was, just humming a song or two.

Pitter patter, pitter patter, Dad sang, and sometimes he got sad and happy at the same time.

He was smiling and there were tears in his eyes, so his eyes were big and wet and shiny.

Mom and Gramma and Grandpa were all working sometimes, so they weren't at home and Dad said, It's me and you, buddy. It's just us men to hold down the fort, so if the Indians or robbers or bad guys come, it's up to me and you.

Sometimes Dad called him a bunch of different names right in a row. Dad said he was Slick. Ace, Butch, Kiddo, Buster, Honey, Sleepy, Doc, and Grumpy.

He was Jack and Harold and Kid Connor.

Anything you want, Dad said. That's how it was way back then, in the Army. You could be anything you wanted. You could be from North Dakota or Indiana or Boston, Massachusetts.

The best days, Dad said, and he closed his eyes and smiled with the pleasure of it. And that was nice.

Sometimes walking to the store with Gramma was fun. Gramma in her big hat and her brown shoes, and her black handbag, and she said, I've got all my money in here, enough to pick up and buy the two of us a train ticket to just about anywhere in these United States.

Where do you want to go, young man? Gramma asked.

California or Florida or upper Michigan.

In California, she said, they could pick grapes in the noonday sun, and in Florida they could pick oranges until the sun set in the west, and the smell was perfume in the air. Or in Michigan—why, a person could go up north where the lakes and ponds were, and hunt and fish all day, then cook on the campfire and sing songs till bedtime. Watch the moon cross the sky right outside the flaps of their tent, and that would be pretty darn good, now wouldn't it?

She patted her black pocketbook and said, It's all in here. I've got it all taken care of. And that was nice to think about. Some faraway place.

Books were usually nice too. Books about a family lost on some island and building a giant tree house. Books with pictures of boats and dragons, and one time a book about a boy tied down on a table, and people in robes, in funny hats—some pointed, some with bells and half-moons on them—moving around the tables, almost singing things in languages he didn't know. That wasn't nice. That was scary, and it wasn't really nice to scare little boys, no matter if it was only done for the fun of it. If it was done as some little trick or joke. Ha, ha.

But most books were very very nice, even when they were sad and a little scary. The one about the lost prince was nice. How when his mother and father, the king and queen, died, how lonely and sad he was.

He couldn't walk either, because of the way he was born and he was put away in a lonely high castle, and almost no one ever came to see him. But then he had a magic carpet he could fly on, and somehow, everything turned out okay. That was nice.

He fell in love with a beautiful princess and he could walk after all, and even though the queen and king were still dead and would never come back to him ever again, he could look at their picture and feel happy and lucky anyway. That was nice too, although every part of the story was not so nice. But as long as the end of the story was nice, and everybody felt good and warm and fuzzy inside by the end, then that was even better.

Sometimes three or four days in a row would go by and he wouldn't be clumsy or stupid, and he wouldn't say exactly the wrong thing at the wrong time. He wouldn't trip and fall, then start screaming, and he knew how that could upset Gramma and Mom, and especially Dad if he had been eating too many hot dogs or chocolates the night before and had one of his really terrible morning headaches.

He would be quiet and he wouldn't be selfish and ungrateful the whole day. Just whining and complaining, and telling those lies of his, and worst of all, sneaking around. Asking for this or that all the time. Always greedy and selfish and thinking only of himself every minute of the day.

It was like he was invisible and silent, sitting in a corner of the living room on the second floor, or lying under the bed playing with shoes — only he'd remember to line them up afterward, just the way he had found them.

No one had to say anything to him, and everyone went calmly about their business. He didn't cause any trouble and put Gramma in a spell or make Dad drink or Mom sad and tired. Mom didn't have to sigh for three or four days in a row, and Grandpa smoked his pipe and never said much, and he, John Connor, felt so good for so long that he practically held his breath, and that was so nice.

It was nice when Mom told about being a little girl, only once in a while she left the sad part out. She told about being left alone in a room all day, with stains on the bedspread and the boiling-vegetables smell, but she would think only of nice things that were going to happen as long as she prayed hard and kept happy thoughts in her head.

How one day, her lost father, whom she had not seen in so long that she couldn't even remember if she had ever truly seen him—how this lost man would finally come back to see her and find her and he was everything she could ever have hoped for.

And this was the good thing, Mom said, and this for him was the best part, the part that made it so nice.

Because each time she kept bad thoughts away long enough, her father would come back and he could be different things each time, with a different story. And when she thought of him, and when she prayed very sincerely and very hard, then she knew that God would hear her and grant her what she truly needed, in the deepest, purest part of her soul. In the part of her soul that wasn't yet stained black.

So he came back each time, in her days in the room when her mother was cleaning people's houses and taking care of their children, she would see him with curly black hair, or with red or brown or blond hair.

And each time a story—of adventure and danger, and always in the end, heroism. How he saved a busload of starving orphans in Mexico from a roving band of robbers and kidnappers, and how he converted the leader of the band to Catholicism. And soon, the whole group of robbers and kidnappers converted, received instructions in the church from her father, and founded an orphanage where there was plenty of food to eat.

So her father had to be away from her and her mother for a time, to make sure everything would turn out nice.

He was sorry to be away so long. But now he was back to stay. Now he would take them to their real house, and their real house was no little room with flaking paint, and a smelly bathroom down the hall.

Their house was painted white and there was a white picket fence. There were trees all around, and green shutters on the windows too. Maybe a car out back, maybe three or four cars. And horses, and maybe a friendly pet dog with floppy ears who didn't bark or growl. Who licked her hand.

His name was Sammy and he was always nice.

Inside there were shiny wood floors and big rooms with lots of light coming in the windows. She walked through the rooms, one after the other, and pretty soon she was a little lost, and when she turned around to look, there was nobody behind her.

She went up some stairs and down more halls, and past closed doors. There were fewer windows, and the house grew a little darker.

Then she went into a room and there was a bed, and her mother was lying on it and she was very sick. A mop and bucket for cleaning were lying on the floor next to the bed. Her mother had a handkerchief tying her hair back, and she was pale, and barely breathing. She was tired and very sad. She had been working so terribly hard for so long and now there was nothing left over. For anyone else. It was all gone. Her energy and now her life.

Mom as a little girl turned away from the bed and looked behind her, and her father was there. He nodded his head sadly and motioned with his hands that there was no hope and that she must pray to the Lord in heaven. That his will be done.

That part was sad, and was not very nice, and then his mother, John Connor's mother, said, And that's when I knew the sad thoughts had come back.

So she combed his hair back from his forehead with her fingers and said there were other, happier stories. How in the orphanage, when her mother gave up and finally put her in there, up in Tarrytown, on the Hudson River, they had a giant pine tree for Christmas, and there was a tiny white light in each window of the orphanage. So when Sister Teresa and Sister Mary Ruth took them outside in the dark, and walked away a little bit and then looked back, it looked like a special and beautiful palace in a fairy tale.

That was nice for Mom, and it was especially nice for him, to know that some nice things had been there in her life too, back when she was his age, way back in the old days. Not just sadness because of not having any family to love her.

There were other nice things too, all over the place, when he put his mind and heart to thinking about it.

It was nice that the sun rose every day and gave them light and warmth. Because of the sun, which God had made in his infinite wisdom and love for his children, life itself was possible.

It was nice that the rivers flowed and the seas teemed with creatures to eat.

It was nice that Jesus Christ, God's only begotten son, was crucified and died on the cross for each of us. He hung on the wall above Gramma and Grandpa's bed, and above Mom and Dad's bed too. He hung over the washing machine in the kitchen on the second floor. At church, which was God's home, he hung just about everywhere you looked.

It was nice to be reminded of all that Jesus on the cross had suffered for us, and without even being asked to.

Maybe the nicest thing was when he fell down the cellar stairs because he was so clumsy and didn't have the common sense to even come in out of the rain. It hurt worse than anything, and it was dark, and he lay there for a long time before he heard the siren. But it was nice how everyone was to him. How they lifted him into the special car they called the ambulance, with the light on top.

And even before that too. How Gramma came down just before the siren noise got very loud. How she knelt down and put her hand on his face and whispered how much she loved him and how sorry she was.

I didn't mean, she whispered.

I'm so so sorry.

I'm a monster.

I should be put away somewhere, she whispered.

Then she said, even softer and lower, Clumsy Jack. Wandering around.

They leave the door unlocked.

Look what you've done.

Sneak around.

Make everybody upset.

Sneak up. Surprise them.

She whispered, Serves you right.

Now you know.

Now you've paid.

Then the men came down with their strong voices, and their uniforms and the special bed to carry him.

The shot pinched, then he felt better than he had felt in the world. Like God and angels singing. Like almost all the pain gone, and this beautiful feeling like he was with everyone in the world, with the stars and the sun and the oceans.

The ladies in white said, Little boy, and they said, Sweet child.

Where does it hurt? they asked. How does it feel?

They said, Nobody will hurt you. We'll take care of you.

He didn't know if it was a minute or an hour or a day or a year. It might have been forever. It might have been all of time gathered together.

The man in the white coat smiled at him. The man took his hand and felt at his wrist, and patted him lightly on the knee and shoulder. The man pressed his belly lightly. He said, Tell me if this hurts.

Then he was in a dark room with the woman with red hair who said her name was Ellen—and she was there holding his hand. They took a special picture.

Then someone else was there, and he was floating and drifting some more, in the warmest, softest water in the world. Deep, still music played, music that lifted and lulled him, music that melted his heart.

Something hurt bad in his arm, but just for a moment. He cried out, almost, but again just for a moment, he thought. Then it passed.

They said, Shhh, and, Hush, and, Little boy.

All of them standing around him, while he lay on a table, only no candlelight, and with funny hats and clothes, but funny in a different way from the book.

Clicks and blips and beeps, and all the time he was high above and far away. And this was heaven, he was pretty sure. This was the most beautiful thing in the world. This was nice beyond any nice he had felt or known.

They called him Possum and Peanut and Pumpkin.

One low voice called him Love.

She said, Okay, Love, and that was him, he knew.

And the sky was so so high, and he had already paid and now they wouldn't hurt him anymore. Everybody would know and he would never have to leave the table or all the people with masks and the white room and the big silver light.

It was all over now because she couldn't help herself anymore. She didn't want to or mean to—and all of them would be mad at him at first but then they would be very sorry.

He couldn't help his eyes and ears and what they saw and heard. And now there was another needle in his arm, and that too was nice, above and beyond the whole world.

Someone with hair like a halo was above him and touched his face, then went over his face with a damp cloth and said all the time in a low kind voice, Little boy. Sweet boy.

Then he was in the white room with the silver light, and they said, Jackie, and he breathed deeply into the funny cone on his nose and mouth, and he was drifting up to heaven.

Little boy, they said. Beautiful boy, they whispered, and that was the nicest thing of all. Sleep and peace.

All of it.

For the rest of forever.

27.

JOHN CONNOR IS pale and seems almost frozen to me, as though he is very tense or numb or removed. His eyes are quite shiny and a very dark blue, and I believe that he has been given sedatives these last few days. So of course he does not seem his normal self, though if you were to ask me, I could not really tell you what the normal John Connor looks like and acts like. What I do know and what I know he knows and has to be thinking about every second now, is that this is his last day on earth. He has less than twelve hours to live.

I will be with him, just outside the bars of his cell, these last hours, or for nearly all of them because there is nobody else to be with him. No family, of course, and no friends or fellow workers or neighbors, and there will be almost nobody to shed a tear for him. He has nobody, and as he has told me, that will not matter because he is nobody. I am less than a speck of bark falling off a tree in darkness, in the wilderness, he said to me, and I said, A speck of bark does not have an immortal soul, and God does not love a speck of bark. He does love John Connor, I said, as lost as he is. As lost as John is, I should add; it is not God who is lost. Though to John, and to many others in our world, God is as lost to them as they are to God. Finally it is a matter of semantics, though it is faith itself that we are talking of.

But perhaps I am wrong. The older I get, and I will be seventy-six this fall, the less certain I am of most things. Even, I'm afraid, of what it is exactly that I believe in. I do believe, but I have less and less of a clear idea of who or what God is and what I dedicate my life to. I once thought of him or it as a white man with white hair and a white robe, sitting on a golden throne in a blaze of brilliant light, surrounded by hovering angels. I thought of him as infinitely wise and calm, and watchful, of course.

But now, if any part of that image rings true, and if God had any human qualities whatsoever, then it seems certain to me that he—if he is a he at all, and that can surely not be certain—he would be unbearably sad and grief-stricken by what he had created on earth. To sit and watch the cruelty and loneliness and suffering would be far beyond any human capacity to endure pain.

God would have to answer for John Connor, for his presence in this cell, and for the life John Connor has led and the things he has done.

What I know instead is that John suffers and will soon be dead, and that the Commonwealth of Massachusetts will have blood on its hands. And of all the states in the Union, this is the very last state I would have expected to see kill a prisoner in its care, even after that bill was passed years ago. No state played a more crucial role in fomenting the revolution and in the formation of the republic, and later, in helping to lay the moral groundwork for the emancipation of the slaves. As the United States is to the nations of the world, so I always thought was Massachusetts to the fifty states. A moral beacon, a city upon a hill. But maybe none of that was ever true, and now that Massachusetts will be wading in the river of blood as well, we can say that barbarism is now quite general over the land. Perhaps it always was.

But I am here, not because of faith or God or because of my disgust with the commonwealth and the nation, but because I am a human being and John is a human being, and if I were him and had his mind and heart and soul, if I had his experience, I may well have done the very same thing. Who ever knows?

Now it has become a state-wide circus, and there are hourly updates on all the radio and television stations. The newspapers have promised special execution issues, as they have chosen to call them. We see the television reporters, their microphones in hand, with their hair, their suits, their good teeth, standing in front of the cameras, putting on their solemn but alert faces, and saying to the anchor back in the Boston studio, Well, Jim, or Gloria or Connie or Lenny, there are only twenty-three and a half hours until officials here at Cedar Junction are prepared to carry out the execution of multiple murderer John Connor, the first person to be executed in Massachusetts in more than half a century. Connor, we're told by prison officials, is calm and seems resigned to his fate. Officials also say that the inmates here at the maximum-security prison in Walpole are calm as well, and going about their normal, every-day routines. Connor has reportedly refused a final meal, and the owners of a number of local restaurants, who offered to cater Connor's last sup-per, expressed disappointment.

They then describe how Connor will be marched into the execution chamber, near the prison's infirmary, shortly after eleven-thirty tonight, for the 12:01 execution. They tell how Warden Daniel Lucas will read the execution order to Connor, and how phone lines to Governor Win-throp Singer will be kept open in the event of a last-minute pardon. The governor, however, has steadfastly refused to offer hope of a pardon for Connor. The courts have spoken, Singer has repeatedly said, and I will abide by their decision.

So John sits now on his bed, and he seems to look in the distance, and when I follow his gaze, I see the clock on the wall outside this cell, and it reads 12:34.

Jack, I say, is there anything you want or need? He just looks at me, blankly, I think, then turns away.

I'm holding my rosary beads, and I say five Hail Marys, followed by an Act of Contrition and an Our Father. I try to keep myself in this place at this time. I can feel all the cinder block and concrete and steel here, and I can feel more tension than usual too, in these always-tense buildings. This feels like a big, momentous event and I can almost sense the hundreds and hundreds of reporters who are hovering over us, and how half the state seems to be waiting and watching. There were even reports of this pending execution in *The New York Times* and on network news programs—because Massachusetts is not the kind of state to execute people, or so many seemed to think.

Coming into the prison is shocking to someone who has never been near such a place. After I contacted Warden Lucas' office, and after John agreed to see me, I had more than a moment or two when I was asking myself what I had in mind. Coming to see a place like Walpole, to see a man who had done what Connor had done. The whole thing struck me as just a little bit odd or strange.

I thought too that Jesus was a prisoner of the Romans, Gandhi a prisoner, Martin Luther King a prisoner.

Another voice said to me that someone who killed three elderly members of his own family as they slept peacefully in their beds, that such a person was not Jesus or Gandhi or King. There was no similarity in any way, shape, or manner.

Then for him to leave the bodies in their beds in the summer heat for a full week, and to live and breathe in that house while his parents and grandmother lay there, was beyond my understanding or comprehension. When I first spoke to Connor, I suggested he try to remember and write down all that he could about his life. Maybe then, in some indirect way, some form of understanding might occur.

Perhaps I knew how strange this whole thing was the moment I first came here. It seemed to freeze some part of my heart to approach these high fences and walls, to see the coiled razor wire on top of the fences and walls.

To go through X-ray and metal detectors, and especially to feel the gates and the heavy steel doors close behind you, with a crash that seems like despair itself, is to lose some of your life. And even though it is only for an hour or two, it is the strangest and most chilling experience of my life.

I tried to think of anything in my life that was remotely similar, and the only thing I could think of that was anything like this was also absolutely different as well. Some thirty years ago, shortly before the time of Vatican II, I went to a Benedictine monastery in the Midwest for a week-long retreat. I arrived very late at night, and I remember a single monk in a long, dark robe let me in at a door in the heavy stone wall, and how silent and dark everything inside seemed. I was led to my cell, a simple room with a cot and a table and chair, and a single small window that looked into what I later learned was a flowerless, green garden that had brick walkways. When I had left my bag, I went out into the hall and down some stairs, then around and down more halls and stairs. I went through a heavy wood door, and found myself in an utterly vast, black space that seemed as huge and dark as some lightless night sky.

I could not see my own hand or arm, it was so dark, but somehow I knew, perhaps in the oldest part of my brain that knew something vestigial about the darkness of caves, that this was a vast space, and a space that was holy.

Then after five or ten minutes, or perhaps after an hour, for time itself seemed to have entered a new dimension here, I began to make out, hundreds and hundreds of feet in front of me, and small as specks, two distinct white lights, flickering slightly, that I knew were candles on an altar. They seemed intensely bright in and of themselves, without illuminating anything else.

Everything seemed strange, and it occurred to me that I had been awake nearly thirty-six hours, had been on trains and buses for more than a day, and that it was probably three or four in the morning. I was in an otherworldly and holy place, but I was also in a weird and holy place in my mind.

Then very low at first, I heard chanting, and the sound was soft and barely audible. Slowly it built, then far off to my left I saw or maybe felt two columns of hooded monks move slowly into the space, reach what seemed to be a center aisle, move toward the specks of candlelight, then part—one line filing to the left, the other to the right, each taking its place on each side of the specks of tiny light.

I could smell incense somewhere too.

The monks were saying matins, the first of the seven sets of prayers in a monastic's day, and the voices raised in prayer and song, the ancient Latin, the dark, the sleeplessness, and the fact that I was witnessing something that had been performed every morning since the time of Saint Benedict, fourteen hundred years ago, gave me a peculiar, out-of-time feeling. And the feeling was as close to the divine, to the oceanic sense of the world as one great body of being, to God himself, I have to say, as I have ever been in my life.

I have thought of that moment often in the decades since. Because at the same time I was very deep inside myself and very far away, and profoundly open to this other world of the vast space in the monastery or maybe in the sky.

In fever I have felt a semblance of that strange place, and once when I had surgery and was given opiates for the pain, I had a similar, if muted, feeling.

That timelessness, that sense of being deeply lost and just as deeply found at the same time, must be at the center of religion, and perhaps for some unfortunate people, of drug addiction too. Perhaps an alcoholic or heroin addict is seeking God too.

I think of that now, with John, and of how far away and close a prison and monastery are. And how in losing John, in his knowledge of his own death, in the when and where and how of it, we begin to understand Christ's long night in the garden at Gethsemane.

By now it is later, is close to the time of supper, and he has stood up, has gone to the bars at the front of the cell, has used the toilet, sat on the cot, looked at his hands, yawned and stretched his arms and legs.

His fingers seem to tremble, and because of the fluorescent light in here that has nothing of daylight in it, his skin seems so white as to be almost blue, and the hollows in his cheeks and under his eyes are black with shadow.

He is wearing jeans and a white T-shirt, and the kind of thin foam slippers hospital patients wear.

Guards come in and out of the locked hallway by his cell, where I sit on a chair. They nod to me, look in on John, then stand for a while at each end of the hall.

An orderly comes to the hall, asks John to sit on the cot close to the bars, and gives him another shot. Then a nurse, a Hispanic man wearing a name tag that says DIAZ, comes in to put an intravenous line into John's arm, just below the crease on his inner arm.

This is as long as death, as quick as life, as exhausting as a day with small children. I have not had my nap today, and I have slept little lately. As the red second hand moves steadily along on the clock on the wall, I think that this will never end.

John, I say, should I pray for you?

He nods and his hands and arms are trembling now, and he stands, sits, squats down, stands, pees into the small metal toilet, lies briefly on the cot.

His pupils are very dark and quite large, and the tape holding the IV needle in his arm seems intensely white, even next to his pale skin.

Holding the rosary beads, I continue to say Our Fathers, Acts of Contrition, Hail Marys.

At seven o'clock, a man in a brown suit comes solemnly into the hall and says, Mr. Connor, Bob Newland of the Corrections Department.

I hope you're doing okay under the circumstances, he says. God knows, this can't be easy for you, or for any of us for that matter.

He asks John if he's changed his mind about dinner. John shakes his head.

Anything at all we can get you? Newland asks. Any phone calls you want to make? Any final requests?

Again, John shakes his head.

Newland turns to me and says, Father, any time you want to give the sacrament, just tell one of the officers.

Then he nods at John and at me, and goes out.

John is wearing the chains, the loose chains, the guards call them. On his wrists and ankles, a heavy leather belt in the middle at the waist, and connected top and bottom so that he can just shuffle when he walks, and move his arms and hands, but only in a limited manner.

The sacraments, I say. Will you make a confession or take communion?

No, he says in a still-quiet voice.

The sacrament of the sick? I ask. Extreme unction, I say.

This time he nods.

I ask the guards to open his cell, but before they do, they unlock a door on the hall, and two more guards come into the hall.

They unlock the cell door, and let me in. They stand in the doorway at my back, and John Connor lies down on his back on the cot, his hands folded on his chest.

In the sign of the cross, I touch his eyes, then his ears, nose, lips, hands, and feet with holy oil, while I pray. In this way, we seal each of his senses from the world.

In every way that he has known, apprehended, and communicated with the world—by sight, hearing, smell, taste, and touch—we symbolically sever these ties. We release his body, so that his soul will be free.

Let us pray, I say, and his hands continue to shake and tremble, and his whole body seems to visibly shudder.

Then I make a final sign of the cross on his forehead with holy oil, and the skin there feels oddly cold and almost waxen.

I go out to the hall, while the guards lock the cell door, then I walk up and down the hall a few times. I am as tired as I have been in a long time. The clock reads close to eleven, and I believe I have been awake since at least four in the morning. And this feels like something weirdly religious and barbaric together.

This is some ritual of bloodletting. A holy and pagan rite of sacrifice.

Now it seems to go slowly but also very quickly. Diaz, the nurse, comes back in, and he gives John another shot of something and says, This will help you relax.

Then guards come in with a large diaper for John to put on under his blue jeans. I turn away, and hear the sound of a zipper, and I pray to almighty God, for his wisdom and peace and understanding.

Then Diaz takes John's arm, and with the tenderness of a mother, he injects a solution into the IV line in John's arm.

This is a saline solution, he almost whispers. To make it painless. To make it easier for you.

He whispers, Good-bye, brother, and I watch him stand and move to the door at the end of the hall.

Then there are four of them, as well as Mr. Lucas, the warden, and I am told to stand directly behind John Connor, and his hands continue to shake and tremble as though he is very cold.

I whisper, Hail Mary, full of grace, and continue to, Now and at the hour of our death. Amen.

I think of my own father and mother. Dear God.

Then we begin to move.

Then

28.

THE HEAT UP there was so bad. Ninety-five, a hundred. The sun on the roof forever, and humidity so thick I couldn't breathe too much, and it went on and on.

There was my Fiorinal, Valium, phenobarb, codeine, Talwin, Dalmane, Seconal. Take two, take two, take two. A coffee, a coffee, maybe a handful of dry cereal to eat, then warm beer and white wine. I had enough to last the whole month of August, there at the end, without ever going out, and they were going to be coming soon anyway to take me back to the ward, and that would be the end of all these years then, and nobody anywhere would ever know about them and what they did and about me and what I did.

Any minute, any hour, any day, they'd park out front or in the driveway, maybe two cruisers this time, maybe four big cops with Mace and cuffs and Gramma with her arms folded and looking, without saying, I told you. I told you.

And I slept and woke over and over. Night, day, dark, light, all swimming around the same by then. And my mind not right because of the heat, the booze, the drugs. They will do that. And just so empty too.

Black birds flying all over in my head. All over, and squealing and cheeping all the time. And I itched too all over, itched like a bastard.

But I had keys to their doors, and I went in very late, and opened the capsules of Dalmane and Seconal, the white powder, ten or twenty capsules, and many small piles of powder, and every night put the powder in their bottles of milk and gin and that bourbon in the brown bottle, Four Years Old or More, it said, and all the time the heat. The terrible insistent heat. My neck, my head.

Oh.

And they were sleeping each in their bed. Old gray hair, and old skin, and shallow breath, and I think for sure: They were growing tired. They knew. They understood this had to end one way or another. Another or one way.

So they knew, I think, deep down, and I kept the lights off, and this was the only way—because of the cops, the years, and how tired, and how long we had all been here. Maybe in the years, me, then Bill, then me—get in a car in the middle of the night, drive away. Get away. Go anywhere but back there. Then go back there, of course, because that was where everything was all along anyway. Where else was there any life or hope to go to? No one can know that but us, and that is the sadness.

How cars went by out front, especially late, and the lights flashed like sudden thunder and lightning. You shake your fist at the sky. You say, Fuck, fuck, fuck. All done everywhere.

So way down they knew, and for night after night I went slowly creeping in on Indian's feet, in through the locked doors like a ghost by then. A ghost of an Indian. Silent, silent. No blip, no bump. No feather falling even. Put powder in, and they slept longer and deeper each night, slept like babies in dreams, when they were so so small and didn't know any better.

Nothing left by then. The clock somewhere ticking loud as death, but nobody anymore could hear, and by then it was so late.

Water dripping in the sink. Creeping cat, barking dog. Maybe dust on the kitchen wall. The calendar there said August 1988, hot hot time. And just a single dim star above in the sky. Hanging dull as a brown leaf.

Thursday, Friday. Another day and night, then another. More minutes and days. And every night the gin and milk and Four Years Old or More bourbon were lower down in their bottles and boy were they tired. Boy oh boy. After all these years, and you think they want to put up with this even a moment longer? Well, my friend. Think again. Think two times even.

Smell like soap and baby powder, and that awful heat. You can't breathe, and when will it end? When will something come along and save us? Stop this? End this once and for all?

How you go around at night. Some creep, like an insect, in the bushes, outside the windows. Go here, go there. Squat down, the eyes big, the eyes shining. Drive a long way. Start here.

In a book, how he had that crooked smile, was shy as a shadow. You can't catch it. Maybe wanted company. Couldn't say.

Momma, Gramma, Dad. Joanie, Bill, Belle. In a house in a place. A room somewhere. Lived and died in a room, and how many rooms in the world, and how many in the city of Newton or Boston, and what happened in them?

Spread their legs, that warm spot, that urge, that urge, then spread their legs again. A baby comes out crying. Wants this and that and everything. Every fucking minute of the day and night. Won't shut up and go away for even two fucking seconds in a row.

So by then. How late? Maybe midnight, maybe two. And by then, oh, it was so hot still, and very early Sunday morning, and they had four, five days and nights of powder in their libations. So they were tired and ready for rest. In their heart of hearts, way down in the bones and sinew, in that pale tissue, the gray creases of the brain, they had to know. To suspect.

This was not in hate but in mercy. I said the little Latin I knew from church when I was very small.

I took pills and itched, and this was deep fog and a form of other

thinking. Beer and wine, and sweat dripping down and all over everything. Down my back and arms and face. Dripping into my eyes, down
my nose.

Who said, I hate you? I wish you were dead?

Said, Don't worry, sweet pea? Sweet little boy?

Said, Just go away now? Just go while you can?

Said, Before it's too late? Before there's no time?

When would time stop then? When you closed your eyes at last and
said, I'm ready to go now? I've been here long enough?

And it was still very hot and quiet and maybe three on Sunday
morning, and there were crickets outside. Some sorry breeze pushing the
hot air slowly from here to there. And down the stairs I went. And down
and down.

The way candles should have been flickering somewhere.

My eyes were used to the dark, and I reached the downstairs hall,
between her door and the cellar door, and I unlocked her door, and closed
it softly behind me. Went past her stove, her kitchen table, a broom
against the wall, a faint crack in the plaster.

And so old lying there in her tired bed and I picked up a pillow and
put it on her face and pressed down gently. Feeling tears fall, too, down
my face with the sweat and if there had been any other way around.
Maybe two or five minutes. Said, Did not mean.

Saw too much maybe.

Hail Mary full of grace, I thought, as though I wore black and had
a white collar. Candles and incense, and by then of course it really was
too late and so far gone. And she was peaceful and I knew in my fingers.
The way the blood always knows.

Then took the pillow off, and no breath left. Her old face, eyes a
little open.

Took underwear and laid it over her face to give her rest, put her
hands, folded, on her stomach, and then stood awhile I guess and didn't
move.

Then a car very far away, and finally I went out and did not lock
the door. Went up.

Thought, What if he or she woke up? Momma, maybe, while I was?

And their room like that. Some shampoo smell, some faint perfume. In their bed, quiet as babies. Her arm flung out. Hitchhiking to heaven.

Sleeping so soft. Like some small child. Take him in your arms, say, Sweet sleepy child. Sweet child.

Went first to his side, with the pillow from downstairs, and pressed gently down again. And the powder made them sleep so deep. He didn't fight me. He must have known how all of this would end and had to come to its conclusion.

And again the candles that were not there and did not flicker, but might have. And incense, and some high ceiling. Some space to soar in.

Then on her side, I pressed again, and she, of the three, kicked weakly, and with her nails at my arms and hands, but she was old too and she had powder in her. And how could she have ever known how big I'd grown and that my arms and hands—the veins bulging there—how strong like stone and force I'd grown?

So this fog had lifted for that little time—and it was all clear and fevered as January mornings, that cold blue sky.

But of course it was still so hot, and I think those tears of mine, they wanted to keep falling and so they did.

I put things on their faces, and folded their still-warm hands, and the house, I don't know.

Was quiet and holy and would remain so.

That week, for that week, maybe I thought I could join them. Some merciful peace and silence at last. The big house sailing its dark ocean alone now. No stars or moon ever again.

Maybe heaven itself would crack open now. But it didn't. Just the usual. The light and dark, cars, cats, a person or two passing out front. More heat, and bad heat, and I lay down.

Then my pills, my booze. I had so much of them. Take three or four pills and sip from a can or bottle, then three or four more. Do this again and again, then it was hard to stand up even, couldn't walk or talk. Make grunting noises, and lie there.

Something slammed my head in with concrete. Big and thick. Weighed ten thousand pounds.

Still birds inside. If you looked in my eyes, looked slow and careful, you'd see them way far in there, flitting around, their great wings beating the air.

I would call, I thought, then I wouldn't. I would join them.

And mostly, it was just this flat, dead thing inside me. With nothing at all left, and all of that nothing was gray as stone and seagulls. Deep fog.

Sleep and all these wild dreams. Going away in cars and riding a horse. Going too too fast. Then their bodies rising up from the beds, and the cloths falling from their faces, and they looked and pointed, and tried to talk, but they couldn't. They couldn't ever say anything mostly but I knew anyway what they would say if they could.

That they knew all along, and didn't they always say as much?

Me creeping around.

And maybe down in the cellar, I could dig a deep hole in the dirt floor. A hole ten or twenty feet deep. Someone in a book dug a hole deep in the cellar, and I thought Gramma and Dad had one too, and I could go down there too. Find a shovel. Push it into the earth.

Then lay them side by side down there and nobody would ever know.

Sometime along there they began to smell, and I made myself eat more dry cereal, and take just one pill, then one, then one.

I moved from floor to floor in the dark. Lay on her couch, down on the first floor, and looked at cracks in the ceiling and kept the lights off.

Went to the second floor, and said, Wanna watch the Sox game on TV?

I sat in the back bedroom on the second floor, on the couch which had its legs cut off, and I said, I saw this interesting article in the paper the other day.

I said, You want maybe a steak for dinner? Fry it up with onions, mushrooms?

No one of course said anything back.

Just give me a minute or two, I said in the darkness, and then I said in a humming way, Give me a home where the buffalo roam and the skies are not cloudy all day.

I said, What about those robes you used to wear? Chanting around and such?

Was that a book? I asked. Did I dream that or something?

Then for a while, I went back to the third floor, and going up the stairs was like going through a wall and into a furnace.

And for a while, too, I cried some more, but for myself, I guess, instead of for anybody else. Cried because now I had really and truly and finally fucked it up, and there was no turning away from this one. Like no going back to anything and what in the name of God did I think I was doing?

So many times, when Gramma took my hand and sat me down at the kitchen table, and was nice as ice cream and apple pie. When she said, Try this, and stood there smiling and saying, Isn't that good now? Isn't that delicious?

And Dad standing in the doorway when I was sick with the flu, and saying, You want me to get you something? You want some juice maybe?

Momma too. Burning something for dinner as usual, and dust and grease in every corner, but saying, This isn't so bad, then just spreading peanut butter and jelly on bread and saying, This is just as good. Drinking milk with it and afterward eating a stack of Saltines and saying, A feast fit for kings, and laughing a long time.

They did that. Ate and sat and then said.

And how long could I stay in there with the smell, and someone eventually would notice. Even with the lights out and the curtains drawn.

The mailman, the old lady next door. The kid who delivered the newspaper. Someone would have to mow the lawn and bring in the mail, and maybe too I could sit them up in chairs, in shawls, in front of windows for the world to see. Even put a burning cigar between Gramma's lips.

Ha ha.

Then crying again because this was all so stupid and I didn't know what the hell I was doing anymore, floating along and the house dark as a cave, on a night at the end of the world.

I said out loud, I'll have the blue one, and I want that tailored and I want to be able to pick that up on Friday for the ball on Saturday, now don't you forget. I will simply not abide excuses.

Oh my God, I am heartily sorry, for having offended thee, I whispered.

Then sometime later, sometime around four in the morning, when the world outside was dead as a graveyard, I picked up the phone and listened to the dial tone for a minute, then some beeping came on, and I thought they would know somehow. I hung up and said, Thank you very much. Thank you, I said, and nodded to the crowd filling the giant hall, all looking at me up on the stage, with love and admiration. Just bathed in their love. So so many.

Thank you, I said. Thank you so much. You're a beautiful beautiful crowd. Thank you very much.

Then I cried some more because I was so grateful to them, to the crowd, then I said, You asshole. You worm. You piece of dust, you, and I punched myself in the face, just over and to the right side of my eye.

Then I took a knife from a drawer in my kitchen, and held my arm over the sink, and drew the knife lightly over the skin on my forearm, and watched a thin red line appear. I did four lines.

I pressed the point into my skin, tried another spot, and another, and there were small circles of red.

Lines and circles, lines and circles.

All this time, they were lying there as quiet as mice. They didn't have a single word to say anymore. They were silent as death, and no matter what I said, they stayed that way. No matter how much time went past.

Light and dark moving in and out of the room. Heat, more heat, enough heat to swell some arms and legs, turn fingers into fat sausages. Turn the skin there, underneath, a little black.

So upstairs again to the third floor, my feet making the boards of the floor creak, and down there, if anyone was listening on the second floor, they would have wondered who was moving around up there, and why in the name of all that's holy was he walking around at that hour like some bat or bird or mouse in the attic, and what could he be wanting and thinking? And hours and hours of that. It would just about make you crazy, I guess.

Then I cried some more and said some prayers, and even said a few more words in Latin that I remembered from way earlier.

And this time I think it was for them and not for me and that is how it should have been. Then I asked if anybody had a few final words to say. Anything at all. It didn't have to be deep or eloquent or anything, but nobody did.

So I went down to the first floor, which was dark as hell still, and by then I guess it must have been way past midnight, and wicked wicked quiet.

I called from there. Dialed 911 and said to the lady, There are dead people at 502 Clifton. Please send someone, and hung up.

I unlocked the front door, and even put on the porch light. Then I sat down to wait, and in a minute or two, the sirens started up, and I listened, and thought that when they got there, that this time it would really mean the end of it. And felt kind of tired and peaceful and happy and sad, all at the same time.

29.

HANDS AND FEET and teeth shaking like some December night without covers, and it'll be a long time before there's warmth again, and that's how they're shaking. And teeth clicking now, and hands rattling against my sides, and the chains, they click and ding along and there must be seven or eight people around me and we're in the hall, and standing in front of the steel door, waiting for a call, an order, and some big black guy the size of a garage door, he's right next to me, says very low, How you doing there? and I nod, shake my head, try to stop my teeth from clicking, even smile a little, think this is a long way from anywhere, and behind me, right behind so I can feel him back there, there's Father saying Hail Mary and so forth, and on Jesus' day in heaven God promised an end and so we have come there now and whatnot, and in your birth is your end, and as it was in the beginning, is now, and ever shall be.

Cold like midnight in January, outside with snow slanting sideways down, and some tube of light over us is blinking real fast, and buzzing a little too. Maybe we wait two minutes, two hours, and finally there's an okay somewhere on the other side of the door, but still we wait some more, and me tired and sleepy as anything but freezing too like I should have long underwear and socks and boots, and some big-ass coat with fur around the collar, and I can feel a little pee dribbling out, and oh shit I think, then it doesn't matter of course, and finally the door opens and Father stays right behind me, and I turn my head to the side and see his old gray head bent over with the years and weight, and he says only begotten son, was conceived, and the angels raised their silver voices, and we can go through now.

We stand in that hall, and it's just tile, and a clock says twenty of, I think, and how long ago, and who did I think and there was a woman there, back then, along about in Colorado, and called me Jack and said, You could stay if you want, you know, and that smile, a crooked tooth on the bottom, and brown eyes, I think I remember, and then someone else, some other woman somewhere, again a long time ago, when I had left, and she smiled also, and she had long hair, soft as combed cotton, as fleecy clouds in the sky, and she said, You can touch me, you want, and that was twenty years ago and I was almost a boy then. Still almost a boy. Skinny like broom handles.

They said a long time ago to go where you want and do what you will, and then there were patterns of leaves on the wall. Maybe from a streetlight shining in the crown of a tree, and air like a kiss, so light and everything.

And I guess now, they give a signal again and we move four or five steps, and stand outside the room, and it was only ever next door to the cell really, looks like a medical room and the table-chair like when you give blood, then get a cookie and juice after.

Father, someone says, and the warden tells him this will be it, and he blesses me, the sign, a touch on the cheek, his tired eyes, the road maps of red and blue lines in his eyes. How far, and he says, Go with Christ, in His Mercy, and so forth, and I say thank you with my lips moving but no sound, and he sees that. Eye to eye. He sees that, then he turns away for the next door down, the seats and the curtains, and they bring me to the table and there's a man in white with the gloves and I sit at first, then some little hum moves it back so I'm flat down pretty much. They do the straps, then take the chain and cuffs and belt off.

Still cold as a bastard, freezing cold, and I can almost see them beyond the curtains, in shadow, and bright as high noon here, and no candles of course or anything. Nobody much looking at me, and they're nervous because this is so new, and they'll have to get used to, and you can get used to anything you have to.

Maybe thirty years ago, maybe thirty-five, and that little boy, he had freckles on his nose, he had eyes, everything beautiful in the world in his blue eyes, and he asked if the monsters would come to get him, to carry him off somewhere, come to his house to get him, come to his room. He asked, Is it dark out? And, Why do I need to sleep? He asked if somebody would hurt him, and if he stayed very small and curled up would he be so small that nobody would see or notice him lying in the dark with his eyes clenched tight.

They were in their beds, but that was so much later and after so many things had happened, but always earlier he remembered in the front room there on the third floor, and light from cars on the ceiling and something shadowy, some creak, some slow shuffling of feet.

Wherein the Commonwealth of Massachusetts has found, the warden reads, and the man in white takes a tube that runs from the box and takes my left arm, the IV, and puts a needle in, and maybe for another minute the warden reads, and the straps are snug, but I think there must be six or seven minutes still, and my teeth rattle and click, and the cold is there but now I am here, and I walked, and have not begged or cried or said a thing, and they are lying in their graves, quiet of course, because nobody will ever bother them again, and that holy ground will grow over with weeds, and someday, a long time later, some kid will go slowly by on a summer's day and see nothing but weeds and trees, and feel wind, see lots of sky overhead like they were never there anyway, no matter how you look at it or what a person could say any longer.

Now the curtains open, and their eyes are back there in the shadows, and on me, and the shaking gets worse and my hands are flapping a little and my feet too I think, and, no, I shake my head, I don't want to say a thing to anybody, and the teeth go click click click real fast, and the little boy was just lying there. Close his eyes, which I do. I close my eyes and I can feel the lights in the ceiling and they are right next to me and the clock when I open them is still moving, the red second hand, maybe a minute or two later though I'm not sure.

He was up there, and that darkness, that shadow in the doorway standing, and she was in the room by then, standing and when I looked, when the little boy looked, I could see the shiny lenses of her glasses, she was smiling down at me, and then I was standing a long time later and she didn't know, none of them knew, but they must have known too, and then the world outside the windows, the lights on in the houses at night, the life they had, all those people, and I hear a click and fluid moving, and so many people having lives, then us and we wanted, but people in living rooms, just looking over and a smile maybe, a hello, and turning away, and somewhere else, in the dark on the third floor, breathing a breath, and the whole time being so far and so long